UNTAMED HEARTS
A HIGHLAND HEARTS NOVELLA

Untamed Hearts

A Highland Hearts novella

Heather McCollum

Entangled Publishing, LLC
2614 South Timberline Road
Suite 109
Fort Collins, CO 80525
Visit our website at www.entangledpublishing.com.

Edited by Theresa Marie Cole
Cover design by Pamela Sinclair

ISBN   978-1503119642

Manufactured in the United States of America

First Edition April 2014

This one's for Julie, my fabulous beta-reader and amazing friend who always has my back (especially against bar trolls). I'm sure within a week you'd be captain of the Queen Siren! Let's hear your pirate poetry. I know you've got some spicy limericks in you!

Chapter One

Will Wyatt, dashing pirate, rescuer of stolen children, next in line to captain the ship *Queen Siren*, sat dismally on the jolting seat of the open wagon as it rolled through another glade of spring flowers and tall grass. He watched Dory, his adopted sister, ride horseback before the Highlander, her new husband, Ewan Brody. The two of them whispering, laughing, and kissing rather turned his stomach.

"Enough, you two!" he groused. "There are children back here who don't need to see that." Three of them. Dory made a face at him and continued to laugh at something Ewan said against her ear.

"I think they are sweet," the twelve-year-old girl named Margery said and scooted a little closer on the wagon seat. It was obvious the child had had a crush on Will ever since she'd boarded the ship with Dory when they escaped from

London.

A snort came from the boy, Stephen. He leaned forward to look between them, leaving the four-year-old girl, Charissa, sleeping in the back of the wagon. "I agree with Will," Stephen said and spit over the side. He'd been surly ever since the slave-trading ship he'd been living on was blown to pieces by Dory's magical lightning bolts.

Bloody hell, if only I had her skill, Will thought. He'd gather a storm cloud right over the sickeningly kissy couple and drench them.

"They've been acting sweet on each other since we left port," Stephen added.

"That's what people in love do," Margery said and looked down her little nose at him as if he were a toddler instead of a boy about her own age.

Will stared out at the never-ending green hills and mountains. He'd never heard so many blasted chirping birds in his whole life. "Bloody racket," he murmured and watched the brown sparrows fly between the trees. Granted, he'd been at sea for the better part of his twenty-four years, but even at port most were gulls and scavenging ravens. These little swoopers twittered along like they were the happiest damn birds on earth.

Dory pointed one out, seemingly mesmerized by its song. She looked honestly blissful. Aye, she'd be happy here in the Highlands. He frowned and ignored the pang of loss.

Dory had been raised as his sister, and although at one time he'd tried to kiss her, she'd made it painfully clear that she thought of him only as a brother. But losing any family member was hard, and the crew of the *Queen Siren* was definitely a family, with Captain Bartholomew Wyatt acting as their chief and father. Aye, part of Will's grumpiness was that he already missed her. He huffed. *But she's damned happy.*

He'd rather have said his farewell back at the port along the Scottish coast, but Captain Bart had ordered him to lay low for a few months since there was a substantial bounty on Will's head. He'd been seen aiding Dory's escape from London. The two of them and Ewan were all considered enemies of the English crown. So Will would keep quiet with them up here at Druim. With King Henry VIII busy accusing his second queen of adultery and courting Jane Seymour, he wouldn't care enough about them to send troops to search. On the other hand, if Will stayed with the *Queen Siren*, he'd have to remain hidden onboard at every port for a long while. Nay, it was best to take a little break from the sea.

He inhaled fully and begrudgingly enjoyed the fragrant breeze. So sweet, free of the human waste and brine smell that infused every port. But still it was hard to relax in such a foreign landscape. Who knew what lurked in the forest? He'd even heard that wolves roamed free in the Highlands. Sharks circling the hull, he'd dealt with before, but wolves on the very ground he road over… He'd have to ask Ewan the best part of the beast to hit to fell it.

The tall pines and old growth trees thinned, making it easier to slip between them until a wide, sunny stretch could be seen beyond.

"Just ahead," Ewan yelled back and pulled Dory into him. He pushed his horse into a run. Dory gave a little scream that tumbled into laughter as they tore through the trees out onto another moor.

Margery strained to see between the thick trunks. "I see

it! The castle Druim!" She was nearly bouncing off the seat.

"Druim," the little one in the back echoed sleepily.

"We're almost there," Stephen told her.

Will concentrated on guiding the two shaggy horses they'd bought from a farmer at the coast and broke out onto the moor. Life at sea hadn't taught him a thing about controlling the beasts.

The sun slanted down between fast-moving clouds that bordered on gray. Ewan and Dory raced on their horse across the huge meadow, weaving in and out of yellow gorse bushes. A village spread out at the far end of the clearing with a towering castle and three mountains behind it.

"God's balls," Will swore beneath his breath at the pristine majesty of it all, making Margery giggle. She still bounced in her seat as her head swiveled all around. They plodded out into the open, the horses picking their way around the low boulders and stepping over clumps of peat. Everything was huge: immense sky, heaven-reaching peaks, and a wide, open field like a sea of spring flowers. The castle, made of gray stone, looked formidable, built to weather the elements and the warring tribes of Scots. Yet the sprawling, little village before it and the people moving about off to the side made the scene look like some fairie kingdom of old.

"It's a fair! Look!" Margery pointed as she stood, balancing in the seat. She squealed. "I've never been to a fair when I wasn't having to pick pockets."

Will squinted against the bright sun that pierced down as the clouds blew off. Children chased each other across the field, and a tall mast stuck in the ground. Girls held ribbons and performed a dance around it.

"It's a maypole!" Margery yelled. Will thought she'd

jump off the wagon right there and start running to it.

"What's a maypole?" Stephen asked.

Will gripped Margery's hand and tugged her back down to the seat. "No falling off. We'll get there soon enough." As if sensing a finish line, the two horses trotted faster, jouncing the seats of the wagon so hard he nearly crack his teeth.

Margery turned in her seat. "A maypole is put up on May Day, and ladies and girls decorate it with ribbons and flowers. It's to welcome summer and pray for a bountiful year. It must be May first."

"Sounds about right," Will said as they continued on. Far off to the right, several men stood around while one hit what looked like a small ball with a thin, curved stick, sending it flying over the field. To the left stood four bales of hay stuck with arrows. An obviously pregnant woman let loose an arrow that pierced the target right in the center. A hulking Scot, who looked very familiar, swooped her up and turned in a circle while she laughed. The others nearby cheered.

Ewan and Dory had reached the celebrating couple and dismounted. Ewan kissed the woman and clapped the man on the back. Aye, it was Caden Macbain, chief of the Macbain clan and Ewan's almost brother. The woman must be his expectant wife, Meg, who was related by blood and magic to Dory. Will watched the two talk and then the large-bellied woman pulled Dory into a hug.

Will chuckled as Dory stiffened before she put her arms around Meg in return. Aye, coming here would be an adjustment for his almost sister. These people, this land, none of it was familiar.

Most of the villagers seemed to be moving in Dory's direction with Ewan getting knocked around in celebration.

"Hmph, I guess Ewan does have people who like him," he said.

"Of course he does," Margery replied and frowned at him. "Master Brody is amazing."

Will smiled at the defensive tone. "Aye, you and my sister definitely think so, though I've seen *a lot* of amazing things, little one." He decided to leave it at that, as most of the things he'd seen were nothing for a child to hear about. He pulled the wagon to a stop near the group.

"Margery, Charissa, Stephen," Dory called, "come down to meet Lady Meg. You, too, Will."

Will stood up, stretching to his full height, and let his gaze roam over the milling crowd. They looked cleaner than most, which didn't mean much, as most of the people he saw lived rather poorly in ports at Tortuga and Port Royal. And there were quite a number of sweet-looking ladies, but just as many frowning papas. All the men wore the Scot's kilt. He jumped down from the wagon and walked up to shake Caden's hand. This warrior was as strong as Ewan but with a grimmer countenance.

Caden nodded to him and glanced at the pregnant, smiling lady beside him. "My wife."

Will nodded to her. "Nice to meet you, m'lady."

"Meg. Please, just Meg. And welcome to our little Mayday festival." She looked at Ewan. "What a perfect time for you to arrive. There's food and games." She looked at the children. "I'm sorry, are you all too tired?"

"Nay!" Margery yelled and then lowered her voice. "I think a festival would be wonderful."

A rumble of a laugh came from Caden. "Well then, feel free to wonder. Just stay within the clearing. Ye don't want to get lost in the forests." He jerked his head behind him to indicate three looming mountains.

Will noticed Stephen studying them and moved over to the boy. "Not a drop of sea anywhere," Stephen grumbled.

Will smiled. "Odd, isn't it?" The boy nodded. Charissa tugged Stephen's hand. "Watch her, lad," Will said as the little girl pulled him toward the polished tree tied with ribbons. Stephen frowned, but Will knew he'd watch out for the little girl as he always had. Hopefully her bubbly happiness would help the boy over his poor outlook.

Will walked amongst the running children toward a table that had been set up with ale, bread, and cheese seasoned with green onions. He reached his arms overhead to relieve the stiffness from the two-day wagon ride. A chorus of giggles caught his attention. Three tasty-looking maids whispered nearby as they watched him. He let a slow grin melt along his lips. "Hello," he said.

One of them babbled quickly in the Scot's language, and they ran off. Hmm… Did no one speak English here besides Caden and his wife?

"*Na pògan!*" called over the din. Will turned to see two young women standing behind another table. One was blonde. The one with dark, long waves of hair spoke a laughing line of Gaelic out into the crowd of men before her. Her tresses were black as a moonless night, the sun catching in the length like streaking stars. Slender arms waved in the air, hawking whatever it was she was selling. Men chuckled and elbowed each other, and she clapped her hands on her cheeks as if she couldn't believe what they were saying, though she grinned heartily. She held up a parchment and a quill filled with ink. No sweetmeats or cakes sat before her.

Whatever she was selling, Will was buying.

He joined the small crowd of men. She spoke more in Gaelic, her merry glance scanning the crowd. Her gaze stopped when she met his. Her eyes were a bluish shade of green. Long lashes fell on creamy skin as she blinked, and then her gaze dropped down his length as if she were assessing him. Assessing *him*? *God's teeth!* He shouldered his way up through the crowd where one man had taken up the quill and marked his name on the parchment. The man then pointed at the raven-haired beauty, and she pulled her attention away from Will to smile on the lad.

Bending forward, she puckered her lips. The crowd erupted in merriment and comments, most of which he couldn't understand.

"Make it good, Fergus!" one called out. Will recognized him as Donald, one of the men who'd helped to rescue Dory and Ewan from London. "No kissing, Ann!" Donald shouted, and the girl with lighter hair frowned at him while the crowd booed.

The man named Fergus bent in and kissed Green Eyes right on the lips for a good count of five, though there didn't seem to be much heat in it. The group cheered, and another man jumped up to sign his name on the sheet.

She straightened and smiled, right at Will. "A kiss for a day of work," she said in accented English. He liked the way her lips smiled on the *S*, drawing out the last part of kiss like a soft hiss. "To help remake a house for the orphans." She let her gaze fall out over the crowd as the man who'd signed last kissed the other girl, and the waiting men cheered. "A good cause," she said in English and then switched to Gaelic.

Her eyes strayed back over to Will. "All strong lads

wanted. Just one day's work for a sweet kiss."

"Since I can't kiss my sister," Donald yelled, "I'll take a sweet kiss from ye, Jonet." He stepped up and inked the parchment. "I'd planned to help ye with the orphanage anyway." He winked at her and leaned in for a kiss. She pulled back after the crowd counted to five. Donald grabbed the quill and signed his name again, his cheeks flushing. "I'll take another of those."

"No hogging Jonet," Ann said next to her and took her friend's place to produce a turned cheek for her brother to kiss, much to the amusement of the watchers. Will grinned at Donald's exaggerated smooch on his sister's cheek and then one on her forehead. "That will be two more days of work, Donald," she called when he backed up. "A total of three." He threw his hands up in defeat and moved away.

The line to sign the parchment was ten deep, and Will got into the back of it. Donald shook his hand and introduced him to several sturdy-looking men with impressive scars. They seemed likeable enough and spoke fairly understandable English. He stepped forward as the line moved, his gaze straying back to the girl name Jonet. His breath caught as he connected with those eyes, again looking right at him. She whispered something to her friend without breaking the connection, and the blonde followed her gaze. Will let a slow grin roll onto his face, one that made the wenches in port practically melt at his feet. A subtle blush came to Jonet's cheeks, and she looked down to answer the smile of the next lad in front of her.

Will frowned, suddenly wanting to punch the fool lad who kissed her soundly. Three remained in line before him. He watched Jonet as she took a sip off her mug and chewed a bit of mint. A man rattled off a cutting phrase in Gaelic, and the last lad kissing her turned bright red.

The devil, he needed to learn this language. He already knew French and Latin and a few words from some of the islands in the Caribbean, but he'd never even thought to learn the Scot's Gaelic.

Jonet kept her gaze away from him until he stepped up. Instead of grabbing the quill, he fished around in the leather bag he had strapped across his chest. He lobbed the pure gold sovereign into the air with a flick of his thumb. It cracked starkly against the wooden table and spun on its end, whirling.

"What can I get for this?" he asked softly, his voice a low rumble meant to coax a rush of heat through a woman. The gold coin wobbled and finally flattened.

She pinkened but held her saucy grin. "Just trading for kisses."

He was already close, close enough to smell the early spring flowers in the wreath on her glossy hair. "Then I'm trading for a kiss," he said low. He'd kissed a hundred women, knew just how to touch, how to stroke. She'd likely swoon from his talent.

Will closed the distance over the narrow table. He slid his hand through the heavy mass of ebony to gently hold her nape as his lips met hers. Mint and warmth and sweet, sweet woman. With a nudge, he slanted her face so that they slid against each other, deepening the kiss. She made a small mewing sound in the back of her throat and opened her lips a crack. It was all he needed.

Will's strategic assault escalated as he tentatively tasted her mouth with his tongue. Would she flee? Instead, the woman opened more, inviting him in, touching him, returning the erotic kiss. Sultry heat coursed through him like flowing fire. The world disappeared as a whirlpool of sensation flooded him. He hauled her closer until she molded against his chest, and still they kissed. Her curves pressed against his hard torso. He could feel her warmth through the thin linen of his partly unlaced shirt.

The hoots from behind him were lost in the sound of his own blood rushing in his ears. He was only half-aware of the lighter-haired girl tugging on Jonet, and slowly, as if gliding up through warm, summer water off an island coast, Will surfaced and broke the kiss.

He held her there, so close their noses touched. Her breath came shallow as if she'd run a race, and he fought to smooth his own ragged inhale. *Hell!* Or rather, Heaven.

One finger at a time, he disentangled his hold on her soft nape. When he looked down, he realized that she sat upon the table. Had he dragged her across? He backed up as she wet her lips, her mouth open, and he almost dove back in for another taste. But as if she suddenly realized where she was, she slid quickly off, the barrier once again between them.

She cleared her throat, her gaze dropping as she scooped up the gold coin. "'Twill buy quite a few boots for the children." She nodded in thanks, and it disappeared into her pocket.

Will waited for her to look up, to meet his eyes. Had he scared her?

"I'm Will," he said and felt the man behind him try to move past. Will held his ground and the man cut over to Ann. "Will Wyatt."

It worked. She had to meet his gaze in order to pretend

the kiss hadn't affected her. In a spine-straightening inhale, she lifted her bright green eyes, connecting with him. His breath hitched at the rich beauty before him. Golden fire radiated out from within the green. She blinked and tilted her head. "Well, Will Wyatt, if ye want another kiss, ye'll have to pledge a day's work at the orphans' home." Her saucy smile resurfaced.

Should he toss out another sovereign? Nay, kissing her out here before a hooting crowd wasn't enough. He would have more. He leaned in and noticed she held her breath even though she kept the mask of a smile. His lips brushed her ear. "What do I have to pledge to get you to swive with me?"

Her inhale bordered on an outraged gasp as she straightened away. He didn't retreat, just met her wide eyes with laughing ones of his own. What type of mettle was she made of? He doubted she was a whore, though she was trading kisses to a multitude of men. An orphans' home certainly sounded like a worthy reason.

His smile expanded as he waited for an answer, and slowly her lips relaxed into a grin. "A lifetime of servitude, Will Wyatt," she said, her tone even, one eyebrow raised. "That's all."

Will chuckled and slapped his hand down on the table. "Aye, you have it!"

Jonet started laughing and called out loudly. "Ho, someone fetch Father Daughtry! Will Wyatt has just asked me to wed!"

Chapter Two

Jonet Montgomery grinned at the dark-haired, strikingly handsome stranger even though her heart pounded out a beat faster than the steps of the sword dance. Will Wyatt. Who was he? He was taller than most of the Druim warriors and just as sculpted, from what she could easily see through his thin, linen shirt, left undone at the top to show an enticing *V* of tanned skin. His features were strong and finely chiseled. A scar along one side of his jaw and a bump to show a one-time broken nose boasted a warrior's life. He was roguishly more handsome than most and possessed a quality that none of the Druim warriors had. He knew nothing of her past.

She shook her head and laughed at his wide, blue eyes. After his outrageous proposition, he deserved to be a little frightened of the consequences. And she could only imagine one thing that would worry such a fearsome warrior...the swaying noose of marriage.

"Is that what Eric needs to do to get ye before the priest,

Jonet? Get up there, lad, and give her another kiss!" Donald yelled out, but Jonet kept her attention on the intense gaze of the stranger. It wasn't a staring contest, but she felt almost tethered to his look, curious as to what shocking thing he might do next. The kiss had been scandalous enough, all hot and wet and slanting. And right there before the crowd. Thank the good Lord he'd kept his proposal close to her ear.

He opened his sensuous mouth to say something but then closed it again. A laugh bubbled from her lips. Had she punished him enough? Aye, perhaps. She winked at him and turned away to greet the next man in line. Luckily, the blemish-pocked young lad just gave her a peck. But next up was Eric.

"Aye, give a Druim warrior another chance, lass," a friend of Eric's called. The man switched to Gaelic. "No kisses for those who don't belong here." The man glanced at the pirate and crossed his arms over his broad chest. Eric grunted and heartily agreed.

Jonet hid her sigh in what she hoped was a kind smile. Poor Eric had asked her to wed with him just a fortnight ago, and she'd turned him down. She'd been married once when she was a maid of sixteen. Machar had been much older than she and died during a raid the following year. Since then, Jonet had been waiting for her grand knight to sweep her off her feet, and guarded against tying herself to another horrible man. Eric was not that knight.

"A kiss for a day's work," she said and leaned forward. Instead of the expected, sweet kiss on the lips for a count of five, Eric slid his hand through her hair, half dragging her across the table. His rough hold pushed her head to the side as he butted his tongue up against her clenched lips. Jonet grabbed his wrists and tried to wrench away, though she couldn't move. She would've kicked him if she'd been before him instead of lying halfway across the table.

With an abrupt yank, Eric broke the attack. Jonet cursed and pawed her hair out of her face in time to see Eric hit the ground on his arse so hard he flipped backward to land stomach-down amongst the tall grass. Jonet held her breath and a hand across her mouth. Will stood beside the table, his hands in fists by his sides. The crowd stood quiet for several heartbeats as Eric pushed up onto his knees.

Will swiveled to look into the hard eyes of the Druim men. "Where I come from, if a woman pulls back, ye let her go."

Hugh, captain of the guard, lifted Eric from the ground. "What goes on here?" he asked in Gaelic. Will looked at him but didn't respond with words, though his hand moved to the curved sword strapped to his side.

"Eric was given the wrong impression," Jonet answered in English and glanced at Will, the one responsible for the wrong impression. "That signing up for a day's worth of work on the orphans' home gave him permission to ravish my mouth." She scrunched her face at Eric even though he was busy trying to glare a hole through Will.

"Ye'll kiss a stranger like ye're tupping him," Eric defended, "but not one of yer clan. And then the rest of ye stand around and let him attack one of yer own."

Caden strode briskly forward with Meg waddling behind him. "Looks like ye had it coming, Eric," he said low. The chief of the Macbains took in the small group that had grown grim. "This is Will Wyatt, second in command of the *Queen Siren* and now a brother to Ewan."

"Ewan?" Jonet asked. She scanned the crowd and saw him walking toward them. "Ewan Brody!" she yelled and circled the side of the table. She and Ann ran up to him and wrapped him in a three-way hug.

Ewan laughed and hugged back. Thunder rumbled overhead though the sun still shone, but Jonet didn't care. Ewan was back and whole. "We've missed you," she said and kissed him loudly. A snap of thunder sounded in the mountains behind Druim, making Jonet jump and several ladies scream as they hurried after their little ones.

Ewan caught her hands and took a full step back. He glanced over his shoulder. "They are just greeting me, Dory." Jonet noticed a beautiful, slender, yet shapely woman with long, curling, blondish hair glaring like she wanted to slice her open.

"Dory," Will said from behind Jonet, the name drawn out in a warning. Jonet thought she saw a small *sghian dubh* in the girl's hand, but then it was gone.

God Lord, was she armed?

Ewan stepped back to the woman and pulled her into his side. "They are my friends, nearly like sisters."

Sisters? Well, they hadn't been tupping friends, true, but she and Ewan had been a little more than brother and sister.

"Jonet, Ann, this is Dory Wyatt Brody, my wife."

"I figured that from her last name being Brody," Ann said and frowned. She'd had her heart set on wedding Ewan one day. Instead, it seemed he'd off and wed a foreign beauty who carried a hidden dagger and had a brother that could kiss a lass's good sense clean out of her head.

Jonet smiled. "It's good to see ye whole, Ewan. Caden wasn't sure when ye'd be back and who," her gaze shifted to

Dory, "ye'd return with." She bobbed her head. "Welcome to Druim, Dory Wyatt Brody."

Dory's face relaxed somewhat. "'Tis beautiful here."

"Aye, ye've caught the Highlands on a bright day," Jonet said, and silence sat for several heartbeats.

"So Will," Ewan said, "been making friends?"

Several of the men watching the drama and introductions snorted. "He was becoming quite friendly with Jonet," Donald said.

"And then yer new brother was making a *friend* out of Eric Douglas," Gavin said and laughed. He pointed to Eric, trudging back by himself across the open meadow to the village.

Caden's frown matched the one Ewan was giving Will.

Will shrugged. "I don't stand for men forcing themselves on helpless maids."

"Helpless?" Jonet said, her eyebrows rising.

Will shrugged. "You weren't armed, and he was stronger than you and without discipline enough to let go." He met her gaze evenly. "Helpless."

Her eyes narrowed. "I was not—"

"I think," Meg chimed in, "that the good men of Druim should work on the orphans' home without the need for Jonet and Ann to provide them with kisses." She squeezed onto Caden's arm.

"Aye," Caden agreed and glanced over the crowd. His voice boomed. "If ye haven't already signed up for a day's work, get yer name on there. No more kisses today." Meg whispered in his ear, and he straightened. "That is," he said loudly, "unless both parties want to." He swooped down to seal his lips over Meg's. The crowd hooted and laughed.

"I'm sorry," Jonet whispered to Ann as they eyed Ewan's bride. She hugged her friend when she noticed Ann's eyes looking watery. "And sorry no more kissing today."

Ann laughed a little as they walked arm in arm to the parchment at the table. Jonet tried not to listen to see if Will Wyatt would follow. "Aye," Ann said. "'Twas the only time Donald would let anyone get close to me."

"I wish I had a brother that looked out for me so," Jonet said, and Ann snorted.

"Ye can have him for a spell."

Jonet turned and nearly smacked into the mountain of male standing before her. The sea pirate had indeed followed. The thought sparked her pulse into another race. She looked up into his face, his chin-length hair a drape around his features as he studied her.

"I did not mean to put an end to all your kisses," he said. Och, that voice, that deep, rumbling voice like pebbles under velvet. "But he wasn't letting you go."

"And I was helpless," she replied, an annoyed nip to her words. She turned back to Ann, who gave her a wide-eyed look. Jonet motioned for Ann to help her move the table and attempted to lift the one side.

"You should carry a dagger." Will followed her, hefting the oak table himself. Jonet's breath hitched as his muscles bulged under the weight, the thin shirt barely containing all that strength.

"I don't need a dagger." She held her skirts to trudge through the dry, winter-dead grasses and new spring flowers toward the village. She passed him to lead the way.

"Can you bring lightning down on a man or sweep him away in a twister?" he asked from behind.

"Ha!" she threw back over her shoulder and kept going. Where? She wasn't sure, but he kept following. She'd lead him to the orphans' home where the table belonged.

"Is that a yes or a no?" His tone was serious.

Lord, how he teased! She turned around to pierce him with her gaze. "Of course not! But those lads there wouldn't have let any real harm come to me. I don't need to carry a dagger around here. Druim is my home."

"They weren't jumping in fast enough," he said.

Jonet frowned and veered to the right, down a path toward the far outskirts of the village that faced the moor. She could hear his footfalls behind her. Och, he was actually keeping up even with the heavy, oak table under his arm.

"'Tis dangerous for a girl to put her trust in a group of men to protect her," he continued, quite insistent about the point. "You should be able to defend yourself."

Jonet pushed open the door to the large, two-roomed cottage that had been vacated nearly twenty years ago. She'd cleaned out all the musty rushes and broken furniture, but there was still much to be done, starting with the leaky roof. She pointed to a spot under a window where the table belonged. He set it down and turned as if to leave. Jonet heard the door click shut. She pivoted and caught her breath.

Will leaned against the only exit, looking even larger in the nearly empty room. The flutter in her stomach wasn't fear, exactly. She wet her lips where his gaze seemed to fasten.

"You could find yourself in jeopardy," he said low.

She swallowed. "From you?" Her gaze flitted to the shuttered windows. She'd led him to an empty house on the edge of town. No one had followed them. They were completely alone. He seemed to be waiting, perhaps for her to realize her foolishness.

He slowly shook his head. "Nay, not from me, but you don't really know that, now do you? And what if I was that Eric lad, following you to this lonely house? Those other warriors aren't here to pull him off you as you say they would."

"He got carried away after watching ye," she said. "Normally, no one would need to be pulled off me." Her heart thumped wildly. From danger or from the way he gazed straight into her eyes, she wasn't sure. He looked like he didn't believe her. "And if I screamed, someone would come running."

He frowned. "Waiting for a knight to rescue you is not a good plan. They tend to be late." He drew a dagger from his leather boot.

Jonet's eyes widened, and he held out his other hand, palm out. "I'm not going to hurt you. I'm just saying…you're too damn beautiful to *not* know how to protect yourself."

Damn beautiful?

He kept talking. "You need to learn to throw this, in case that knight doesn't show up when some slimy letch decides to have a go with you." He snapped his wrist and sent the small knife tumbling through the air. It pierced the table with a *thunk*. "I'll teach you."

"I…"she started but had to inhale around the narrowness of her throat. "I need to get back."

He immediately stood aside and opened the door for her. His heat slid across her arm as she grazed him on the way out, and she inhaled on instinct. Clean, fresh, minty with a hint of spice radiated from him. It was already familiar to her, beckoning her. *Foolish!* She stepped briskly from the doorway. She heard his boots grinding into the pebbles behind her.

Jonet pivoted. "Are ye following me?" Och, he was more gorgeous every time she looked at him. The sun shone down between the cottages to glint across his dark brown hair. She blinked.

Will turned in a tight circle. "It's either follow you back to the festival or wander aimlessly through a mostly deserted village that I know nothing about."

Jonet pursed her lips and turned as her face flushed hot. She spotted Ann coming across the field with a small parade of children. Ann waved and then let the littlest one, who had started to wiggle, slide down. The wee lass had reddish curls and ran toward them, her smile bright.

"Will! Will!" she called and flew past Jonet to clasp Will's legs. He chuckled and scooped her up to place her on his shoulders. She latched onto his head, her legs crossed at the ankles under his chin.

Ann caught up with the older boy and girl. "Will Wyatt, yer children were looking for ye."

"Children?" Jonet glanced between them all. None of them had his eyes or the slope of his nose. "These are yer children?" The older ones were nearly half the man's age.

"Ho now, I didn't sire them. The little one kind of latched onto me." To prove the point, the wee lass on his head squeezed her legs. "She definitely needs a papa." He laughed.

"I'm not really a child anymore," the older girl said with a frown. "I'm twelve and so is Stephen."

"And ye are?" Jonet prompted.

"Margery. And if I'm anyone's child, it would be Dory's as she's the one who helped me in London. Stephen belongs to Ewan because he rescued him from *The Raven*."

"More like threw me overboard," Stephen grumbled.

"But Dory," Margery continued, "sent us to make sure you weren't getting into trouble." The girl gazed pointedly between Will and Jonet. Jonet swallowed silently. Did Will have a habit of getting into trouble with lasses?

"Just heading back that way." Will trudged past her with the wee one leaning over his head to drape her curls into his eyes.

Ann elbowed Jonet as they followed. She jutted her chin out toward Will's backside as he walked. "*Brèagha.*" Ann giggled softly, though Jonet doubted he'd understand her friend's appreciative observation of his nicely toned arse. She snorted but continued to watch him walk with all the swaggering ease of a pirate, one with a beautiful wee lass who seemed to trust him completely. Children and animals were excellent judges of character. But if Will Wyatt was so trustworthy, why then did he make her heart pound like she was being hunted by a wolf?

As they neared the festival, Jonet noticed the rather large figure of the priest talking and nodding to Caden. The pious man seemed to be enjoying the spring festival.

Meg turned and smiled at them as they walked up, her hand under her large belly. "Jonet, so glad Ann found you. Father Daughtry is here, and we need to talk about the wedding."

Chapter Three

Will stood at the bottom of the winding stone stairway in an alcove off the great hall of Druim castle. He squeezed Dory's hand where it draped over his arm. "You know it isn't official until the priest gives his blessing," he said with a teasing grin. "I can sneak you back to the *Queen Siren,* and he'll never find you."

Dory huffed, but joy sat heavy in her tone. "He found me once; he'd just find me again."

Will smiled fully at the sweet, simple happiness in his almost sister's voice. He'd never heard her so blasted pleased before.

"Besides," Dory said, "Ewan and I are already wed. Just making it official with the church."

"I know the captain would wish he was here to see you in all that finery," he said close to her ear. She looked at him, her eyes a bit glassy. "But I'm glad to escort you in his place." He kissed her cheek.

Dory smoothed the beautiful blue gown she wore, a gift from the Lady Meg. "Just don't let me trip and fall on my face in front of all those people," she said, peeking out of the alcove.

"My last job of looking out for you," he teased. "I'll get you down the devilishly tricky aisle and then you're all Ewan's problem."

She glared at him, but her eyes danced. Aye, she was thrilled.

As they entered the vaulted hall that Jonet and her friend had decorated with spring flowers and sweet-smelling herbs, Will scanned the crowd for those emerald-green eyes. Jonet stood beside Meg, but where Meg stared with a broad smile directly at Dory, Jonet's gaze met his own. Having been caught, he thought she'd look away. When she didn't retreat, a grin spread across his face. She was brave for a sheltered Highland girl.

Vows exchanged and country minstrels playing, Will stood watching the villagers dancing in long lines. Jonet had ducked outside with several of the ladies who were apparently sprucing up Ewan's little cottage. A few other maids cast appreciative glances Will's way. He gave two lovely ones his seductive grin, which sent them giggling, but then he turned to scan the room once more for dark tresses that seemed inclined to curl. Jonet hadn't returned yet.

When the song ended, Will walked over to where Dory stood over a large book while Meg talked excitedly.

"This is the family lineage that Uncle Harold sent when he returned to England. His mother, my grandmother Joan, was a Mereworth, sister to Edward Mereworth, who was your grandfather on your mother's side," she said to Dory.

"We can fill your name in right here," she said, pointing.

"So..." Dory drawled out, "we have the same great-grandparents?"

"Aye." Meg nodded with a huge smile.

"Did they have the dragonfly birthmark?" Will asked. Will remembered the little brown shape on Dory's wrist from the time she was a baby. Ewan had explained during the journey that the women healers in the Munro and Macbain families all possessed the dragonfly mark.

"My mother did," Meg said. "And Dory's mother did. I'm assuming that it came through our mother's lines as males don't inherit the ability."

"None of them?" Will asked.

"Not that I'm aware of," Meg answered.

"Our great-grandmother," Dory said, leaning over the old pages of the book, "was from Denmark?"

Meg nodded. "Margaret of Denmark was wed to Olaf."

"Sounds like a Viking," Ewan said, and Meg nodded. "My bride is rather uncivilized, lots of plundering."

Dory glared at him, but he caught her in a kiss.

"Where did the rose ring come from?" Will asked and studied the family tree, etched carefully in a slanted, woman's script.

Meg pointed to both sides of the page. "There were two, one handed down to my mother, which Boswell took from her." Her smile faded. "The other one was made by Cromwell, and Dory's mother stole it to prove he was a traitor. My uncle Harold said the rose ring in our family was from his father, Richard Brindle. He has always alluded their father was a secret Plantagenet who was hidden away from his true mother, Isabel, a Lancaster Plantagenet."

"I wouldn't show this to Henry VIII," Ewan said, studying the lines. "Dory's grandmother looks like a Yorkist Plantagenet, and Meg's grandfather was a Lancaster Plantagenet. With that background, the Macbains, Munros, and Brodys could rule England." He looked at Caden. "Ye might want to burn this."

"Never," Meg said and snatched it up, rolling it securely. "It will stay safely with me to be passed on to our children." She moved her hand to her round belly.

"I'll never let it out of Druim," Caden swore, and Ewan nodded, both grim.

The old man playing the tabor drum in the corner rapped out a steady, slow beat, hardly a toe-tapping, celebratory song. It rather reminded Will of a funeral dirge, bringing down the festive atmosphere. What a shame if Dory didn't dance at her own wedding. He grabbed an unclaimed tankard of sweet, Highland ale and wound his way through the crowd.

Three dowdy-faced, grizzled, old warriors sat near the minstrels, trying to tap along. The one with an eye patch yelled something at the trio in a surly tone. He reminded Will of old Pete on board the *Queen Siren*.

"That beat is about as fun as dead sails and a long way to go," Will commented and took another swig.

"Aye, 'twill be a long night indeed unless Humphrey kicks it up," one-eye said. He looked to Will. "I'm Old Kenneth. They are Bruce and Angus. We're council to The Macbain."

"Will Wyatt," he gave his name with a nod. He set his tankard on the cool hearth mantle, grabbed another ale, and headed toward Humphrey.

"Care for a drink?" Will asked, and the man licked his lips. Sweat sat on his round forehead. "I'll take over the drum for ya."

"Do ye know how to keep a rhythm, lad?"

"The wenches have never complained," Will answered, and the man burst into loud guffaws. It sounded like he repeated Will's boast in Gaelic to the two others, and they joined in the mirth, giving the dancers a break while Will took Humphrey's stool.

Will stroked his palm over the tightly skinned drum. It was several hand lengths wide with tall, wooden sides. He was used to playing two smaller drums held between his thighs on the *Queen Siren*, but he could find a rhythm with just one skin, plus the wood sides. The other two musicians watched him.

"Let's see if you can follow this," he murmured and started to tap on the drum with a roll of his hands, striking with the edges of his firm fingers. He picked an easy, quick rhythm. The three old warriors moved closer and nodded as the lute and pipe players began a lively tune. Will grinned with them. *Much better.*

"That's got a pulse to it," Angus yelled above the song.

Dory smiled broadly at Will from across the room, and he let loose with a more elaborate beat that would fit in with the other instruments. Playing was as easy as breathing to him. He'd been playing the drum since before Captain Bart had found him half-dead in the hull of a slave-trading ship. Once he was well enough to sit, Captain Bart said he beat on anything that would make a sound. His new father had placed him before an island drum, and he'd been thumping out rhythms ever since. Captain Bart called the music Will's own brand of magic. All he had to do was start playing, and the crew's squabbles would turn into a round of dancing and good-natured boasts about who could keep up with him.

He closed his eyes and let the varying pitches and side pats encourage the other two men to keep up. One laughed behind him, and Will kept going, enjoying the familiar heat in his arms from the movement. Someone in the room whooped, and he opened his eyes to find the room swaying. Most were performing a country jig, doing their best to keep his pace while laughing. Those not dancing were stomping their feet. Dory had raised her heavy skirts and was showing Ann, Meg, and a few other ladies how to roll quickly between their heels and toes. Meg plopped down in a seat but kept rolling her little feet while several others hopped with Dory.

Ewan and Caden watched with grins and tapped their own toes. "Ye know how to liven up a wedding," Old Kenneth said and danced a little jig himself. Will kept going, at ease for the first time since they'd arrive the day before. Maybe staying on dry land for a while wouldn't be as hellish as he'd thought.

Several children ran through the middle of the dancers, performing their own version of the jig. Margery took Charissa's little hands, and they spun around together. Will looked toward the entry alcove. Large green eyes, framed by shining, midnight-colored hair, looked back. The woman's luscious lips turned upward in an appreciative grin. Jonet Montgomery. The name rolled around in his mind like premium whisky warming his gut.

She tilted her head slightly, and her gaze shifted to his rapidly pounding hands. He almost slipped out of the rhythm as his throat constricted. *Bloody devil.* It was as if he were a nervous whelp performing for a girl he was sweet on. He shut his eyes and refocused on the tune coming from the pipes and lute. Little by little he slowed, signaling the end of the song to the two other musicians. The dancers would surely need a drink. With one final run through the rhythm, Will pattered out, ending with one big slap.

"*Mór!*" the third old warrior, Bruce yelled. "Grand! My heart's thumping like I've been filching cattle from the Davidsons!"

"Ye haven't done that in years," Angus said breathlessly.

"Perhaps I best sit down then." Bruce flopped back onto a stool by the hearth.

Will's gaze followed Jonet as she joined Meg's group on the other side of the room. A number of the children ran up to her before hurtling toward the kitchens, probably in search of some sweets.

"She's bonny, ain't she?" Old Kenneth said beside him.

Will nodded. "Do all those children belong to her? I didn't think she was married."

Old Kenneth took his measure. "Nay, not married any longer. Her husband died in a raid years ago. She takes care of the stray wee ones in the village. Is why she was trading kisses yesterday. I believe ye remember that."

Will met the old man's eye. "'Tis impossible to forget." They stared at one another for a long second.

"Since Jonet has no one by blood here, the council and I, along with The Macbain, consider ourselves her family," Old Kenneth said. "And we watch out for our family." The old man was actually threatening him.

"Good," Will said. "The woman doesn't know how to throw a blade. She needs protection."

Old Kenneth snorted. "Ah now, the lass is strong in spirit." He tapped his chest. "She survived being kidnapped by an ogre last fall by feigning sleep."

"Is the ogre dead?" Will asked, his voice as firm as his gut.

"Aye, had his throat eaten out by a wolf."

"Lucky for the ogre. My revenge would have been more painful," Will said low, and Old Kenneth chuckled. Will's gaze rested on Jonet's straight spine. The green costume fit along her waist and flared out at the hips into full skirts. A white bit of lace peeked out over her slippers. Her legs were probably long, shapely, and naked under those layers.

"Just keep in mind," Angus said, having listened to Kenneth's warning. "We won't put up with a scoundrel tricking his way into any of our lasses' beds."

Dory said something, and Jonet turned and caught Will's gaze. Aye, he wouldn't be tricking his way into just any of the lasses' beds at Druim. Only one bed would do, and it belonged to the unattached, strong of spirit, young widow, Jonet Montgomery.

"Warning taken." Will grabbed his tankard from the hearth shelf and walked over to the ladies.

"Nice rhythm, Will," Dory said, and the other ladies spoke over each other with compliments. "The *Queen Siren* must be quite dull without you playing there."

"Pete will make do." Will sipped some more of the honey ale.

"I was surprised," Ewan said and slipped an arm around Dory, "that ye didn't bring yer drums." Ye played nearly every minute on board when ye weren't hoisting sails and winding rope."

"I didn't think I'd be staying long enough to miss them," Will answered. Jonet's grin seemed to sink a bit, and she turned to grab a tankard off the table. Charissa came tearing through the room, laughing as Stephen chased after her. She wove between the people and swung around Will's legs.

"I don't think she's going to let you go back," Dory said as Will lifted the squirming four-year-old onto his shoulders, out of reach of Stephen's tickles.

The boy handed a small square of raspberry tart up to her. "Oh, we're going back," Stephen said, his smile souring into an immediate frown. "We're pirates, and pirates don't take to land for long."

Will laughed, and Jonet frowned at him. "I can't believe ye're encouraging the lad to be a pirate."

"They are good pirates," Dory explained quickly.

"Actually, not pirates at all," Ewan corrected. "The crew of the *Queen Siren* rescues children from slave traders."

"Aye, but we live like pirates," Will countered proudly. "The best parts anyways."

"Best parts?" Jonet snapped. "Would that be raping, killing, and stealing?"

Dory, Ewan, and the rest flipped glances between them, but Will had never minded an audience, especially when he was being clever or wicked. "I was thinking more of the dancing, cursing, and whor—"

"What Will means," Dory cut in, "is that we enjoyed the freedom of sailing around the world, helping those in need without all the responsibilities that come with living in polite society. Isn't that right, Will Wyatt?"

The last question hissed through Dory's clenched teeth. She only called him by his full name when she was about to lose her temper. He exhaled long. She was trying to fit in with these people, her new crew, so to speak. And his jests to spark fire in those deep green eyes weren't helping.

"Aye, quite right, Pandora Wyatt Brody. Though, I'd also say you miss wearing britches and climbing the rigging, now that you're living in polite society."

"I don't mind if ye wear britches," Ewan said and kissed the side of Dory's neck. That brought the color and smile back to her face.

Will grinned. "Now if he starts making you climb his rigging—"

"Will Wyatt!" she yelled, and he laughed outright. Caden chuckled, and several of the ladies tittered. Jonet's face even relaxed, though the smile was still missing. Charissa started to squirm on his shoulders, and he lowered her to the fresh rushes where she ran with sticky hands toward Stephen.

Bruce called from across the room and motioned for Will to come back for another song. "Seems I have another rhythm to set." The two comely girls who'd flirted with him before giggled and rocked up onto their toes. He nodded to the small group, his gaze touching on Jonet's lovely form. Before he turned away, he caught her eye.

"The green of your costume brings out the emerald in your eyes. Reminds me of the deepest seas under a pure blue sky." Before she could speak or curse or flash him another frown, he pivoted on his heel and headed back to the hearth. Not a one said anything behind him. A grin curved his lips as he felt the heat of stares on his back. He always liked to leave a group speechless.

• • •

The morning had flown by with the wedding preparation, the ceremony, and the feasting. Ewan's bride seemed a bit overwhelmed by the quick plans, but once Meg had set the request before Jonet, Jonet had hopped right to organizing the event. She loved to coordinate celebrations. Father Daughtry was planning to leave as soon as Meg's bairn was born and blessed, so there had been no time to delay in formalizing the union as Meg's time could come any day. Ewan and Dory had already declared themselves wed before God weeks before. So the priest had been swayed to waive the banns after he talked with her and Ann about not having entered a previous betrothal with Ewan. Neither of them had, much to Ann's disappointment.

Jonet sat in the shade of the soon-to-be new orphans' home and looked out over the moor spread across to the forests surrounding three sides of Druim. The four children currently in her care were being watched at the celebration by Ann, so she could take some time to herself.

Jonet breathed deeply and let her gaze stray to the place her table had been set at the May Day festival. Where the huge, handsome, and hedonistic pirate had completely scattered her reason with his inappropriate kiss. Her finger strayed across her bottom lip. She could almost remember the press of his mouth against hers. *Och*, it had been too long since she'd been given a good kiss. Actually, she'd never been given one that made her so hot inside she thought she might catch the wild gorse on fire under her feet.

And then that comment about her eyes just an hour ago. She glanced down at the green dress. Did her eyes really look like the deepest of seas under a blue sky? She'd never seen the sea. Her heart thumped, and she felt her face grow warm, remembering the way he'd looked at her before he'd swaggered off to rejoin the musicians. Heat and promise had mixed with a look of determination.

"Don't fall for him," Dory had warned her as Will took his place behind the drum again. "Though his heart is golden, I've never seen him faithful to one woman."

Jonet frowned as she plucked a wild flower and shredded its petals. She'd guessed as much, but hearing it confirmed made her stomach hurt.

"Here she is!" Charissa's red-gold curls bobbed as she ran breathless around the corner to plop down next to Jonet. "What are you looking at?"

Jonet smiled down at her, though her gaze watched the edge of the building. "Just looking out at the grass waving in the wind. Sometimes I catch sight of a pair of wolves that keep watch over Druim."

"Wolves?" The girl snuggled closer to Jonet.

"They are nice wolves. Umm…was someone looking for me?"

"You disappeared." The familiar timbre kicked at her heart, sending it flopping. "Alone and without a blade," Will added as he walked around the corner.

"How do ye know I don't have a blade?" she asked. Her breath stuttered in her throat as he dropped his gaze to run her length.

"Unless you have one strapped under those skirts, you don't have a blade."

"Jonet says there are nice wolves that sometimes play on the moor," Charissa chimed in, oblivious to the tension.

"Wolves don't play," Will said without taking his eyes off Jonet. "They are wild like sharks, little one." He glanced out at the moor. "Another reason you need to learn to throw a blade."

"Stephen says I'm not old enough," Charissa pouted, leaping up to grab Will's legs.

"Not you," he smiled down at her and rubbed her back. "Not yet anyway. I meant m'lady Jonet."

Jonet stared at the little girl, clearly adored by the stealing, smirking, kissing pirate.

"Oh, do teach her!" Charissa said, tipping her head so far back to see Will's face that she would have fallen if he hadn't held her.

Will looked back to her, an indulgent smile curving his lips. He raised his eyebrows in question.

Jonet pushed up and dusted her skirt. "I don't have a knife to practice with."

Before she'd even finished shaking her head, Will flipped his wrist, and a blade whirred through the distance to *thwak*, point first, into the frame of the door by her shoulder. She jumped but managed to hold onto her gasp. Charissa giggled.

"'Tis for you," Will said.

"I won't take yer weapon," Jonet said and looked at the sleek, black handle protruding from the wood. The small dagger was a *sghian dubh*, a deadly little blade that could be secreted away on a body to be retrieved quickly when needed.

"'Tis not mine. I bought it in the village for you."

She looked back at him. "I don't take gifts from… strangers."

"Are we strangers?" He grinned wickedly. *Och*, just a simple teasing look and the man loosed lava in her face. He shrugged. "Plus, I'd like to see the gold I *stole* from a slave-trading ship used to protect the helpless."

There was that helpless word again. He said it with enough smirk that she knew he was trying to infuriate her. "Very well then, I will let ye teach me to throw the *sghian dubh* if ye help put a new roof on the orphans' home."

"Skeean dew?"

"Aye, the little dagger." Jonet gestured toward the black handle in the door frame.

Will rubbed his chin where a small beard grew. He kept it trimmed short, but it gave him a villainous look. He hauled Charissa up into his arms and walked around the structure as if seeing how much work would be involved. Jonet snorted and backed up to look at the roof, hands on her hips.

"Well?" she asked.

He held up a hand for her to wait as he continued his inspection, as if he truly was calculating how much effort he would have to trade. She shook her head with a broad grin. The man was infuriating, but he could surely make people smile despite their opinion of him.

He rounded the corner. His gaze connected with her, and she forgot to breathe. She couldn't look away, couldn't move. Such intensity sent a chill along her arms, yet she felt flushed at the same time. "Aye," he said low. "It's a deal, Jonet Montgomery. I will put a new roof over your lovely head, and in return, you'll allow me to teach you to save your lovely head."

Jonet swallowed and nodded, breaking the spell.

"Is that a wolf?" Charissa gasped and pointed. Will pivoted, and Jonet stepped out to look past the house.

"No," Will said, "it's a horse carrying a man."

Jonet held her hand to her eyes against the slanting sun.

"Riding like the devil was chasing him," she murmured.

"*Na laoich*!" a man yelled from the direction of the watchtower along Druim Castle's surrounding wall. "A Davidson!"

"Davidson?" Jonet murmured.

"Who are the Davidsons?" he asked.

"The last leader, Gilbert Davidson, helped Rowland Boswell try to destroy us. The bastard nearly killed Meg before Caden killed him. Their clan has been trying to select a new chief since last autumn."

"So 'tis probably not a friendly visit," Will said, a lethal tone sharpening his usually teasing voice.

"I couldn't say."

"Will, what are ye doing out here?" Ewan said as he and Dory came around the corner. Ewan's gaze fell on the blade sticking in the door frame.

Good Lord. Jonet tensed. She hadn't yet had time to talk with Ewan about the orphans' home.

"Do you know you have a Davidson riding toward Druim like hell's hounds were slobbering on his heels?" Will asked. He passed Charissa off to Margery, who'd come with them.

"Ewan," Jonet started and paused. "I meant to talk with ye before, but with the wedding—"

"Why is there a *sghian dubh* piercing my mother's old home?" Ewan asked low. Dory wrapped her hands around his arm. She must know of Ewan's past, about the night, when he was a boy, that his own father murdered Ewan's mother, the night Ewan had thrown a black-handled blade to strike his father dead. The house had been abandoned ever since, no one wanting to risk the bad blood spilled within.

Jonet felt Will beside her as if he were facing off against Ewan. Which was ridiculous since Ewan was a trusted friend, though he did have murder in his face at the moment.

"Caden gave me permission to use it to house the orphaned children. So many come to Druim now that people have heard about Meg. I can't keep them all in my cottage."

"Evil dwells in there," Ewan said.

Jonet shook her head. "The evil is gone, Ewan. It is just a sad, old house that needs some love and the innocence of happy children to bring it back to life."

The sound of running men filtered between the other dwellings up the street. "Now's not the time to discuss this," Will said, his voice as firm as Ewan's face. Will walked over and yanked the black-handled blade from the wood and resheathed it. He looked to Jonet. "I'll hold it until I teach you not to slice your fingers off."

"The *sghian dubh* is yers?" Ewan looked pointedly at Jonet.

"Ewan," Dory said and pulled his arm. "Let's see what's going on."

The rider had reached the edge of the village and slowed. The four of them, and Margery holding Charissa, ran to the rear of the assembled Druim warriors. Stephen shuffled up, too. Jonet noticed he had raspberry tart smeared around his lips.

"Ho there, Davidson!" Hugh, the one-handed leader of Druim's tower guard called as Caden stepped up to the horse. The man practically lay across the frothing steed.

"What is this about?" Caden asked and held the horse's bridle.

The Davidson pushed up in the saddle. His face looked

pale, grayish-green. "I've come to warn you," he said and swallowed. His gaze slid over all of them but stilled when it fell on the children standing with them. Remorse flicked across his face, and he coughed into his fist.

"Tell us, man!" Hugh urged.

He nodded and looked to Caden, The Macbain. "They are coming."

Chapter Four

"Who's coming?" Caden asked.

"All of them," the Davidson panted. "We couldn't stop them. There's too many." His eyes shifted to Meg as she waddled down the lane with Ann holding her arm.

"What are they saying?" Will asked near Jonet's ear, his breath a feather against her sensitive skin. She quickly translated for him.

"Who are coming?" Will asked loudly.

"The sick," the Davidson answered in English, and a chill ran down Jonet's spine from her nape all the way to her ankles.

"Sick?" Meg asked. "Who's sick?"

The man continued in English. "Most of our clan. The mothers," he paused to breathe, "they are bringing all the children and most of the rest. Some of us tried to stop them. They will infect all of you. But they won't listen."

Meg looked at Caden. "If it was my babe, I'd find a

healer, too."

Charissa sobbed beside Jonet, and Margery shushed her, but Stephen pulled her into his arms. "Will we kill them?" Charissa asked softly. Stephen looked to Jonet beside him, his face clearly showing that he worried about the same atrocity. She blinked at the horror of the idea.

"Captain O'Neil," Stephen said, "whose ship we were on. If someone showed they were sick, he'd have them thrown overboard so the crew wouldn't be infected." The boy shrugged. "The only thing he was ever afraid of was sickness."

Jonet's stomach twisted at the tortured look in the little girl's face. The boy's, too, though he tried to look stern and strong. She shook her head. "Nay, we will help the sick, not hurt them." Jonet felt a warm body step up behind her, supporting her. Without looking, she knew it was Will–aye, a pirate, but a good pirate compared to this O'Neil monster.

"They come to be healed," the Davidson continued.

"I will help them," Meg said.

"How many are there?" Caden asked, his stance strong as if he faced a battle.

"A hundred perhaps."

Caden turned to Meg. "Ye can't heal that many, not even some, not with the bairn in ye."

"I can help," Dory said. "I can heal like Meg."

"There's too many," Ewan said.

"I'll help the worst ones first, and the youngest," Dory said.

"And we can ease their discomfort," Jonet piped up. "Fiona has herbs. We can lay them out in the orphans' home."

"We need to get the healthy children out of here," Will

said. "Where can they go?"

"I'm taking Meg to Munro Castle," Caden said. Meg opened her mouth as if to protest, but then her hands went to her large belly, and she nodded, lips tight. "They will take in all of us if needed. I'll send Rachel back to help. She has the gift as well."

Will glanced around at the standing warriors. No one was moving. "When will they get here?"

"They left just before me," the Davidson said. He coughed, the wheezing changing his pale skin to a flushed red. Several of the warriors backed away from him. Caden went to Meg. "But they are moving mostly in wagons or walking."

Ann's hands held her cheeks. "Walking? Poor people."

"Then we need to get going," Will said. "Now." He slapped his hands together as if he were standing on a deck, ready to lead his crew into battle.

"Aye," Caden yelled. "Hugh, sound the battle alarm to get people into the castle or their own homes. Gavin and Kieven, hitch all the wagons we have and ready the horses with the lads in the stable." The men began to run off as Caden took the lead, issuing orders to pack up the entire village.

Will grabbed Jonet's hand. "Stephen, we'll load up our wagon, too. Make sure we don't lose Charissa in the mix."

Jonet snatched her hand back. "I can't leave. I have to stay to help."

Will turned to her. "You have to keep the children calm, take care of them at the Munro's. You are their mother." He looked intently in her eyes. "Don't abandon them."

"I…" Her lips squeezed together as she considered the

truth of his words and finally nodded.

He grinned then, a look of relief marking his face, and continued to pull her through the busy streets. "Good, else I'd have to carry you over my shoulder."

She huffed at his threat. "I have to get the children's things from my cottage," she said and pulled him to follow her along a winding road. Margery ran behind them, and she caught the girl's hand. Margery's fingers wound tightly with hers. *Och*, the girl was scared. "It will be all right," Jonet promised. "And Dory will heal ye if ye get sick." Margery nodded and followed her into the small cottage as the warning bell rang out.

Jonet pointed to a stack of wool blankets folded by several beds. She looked at Will. "Take them to the orphans' home. Ewan can lay the ill out in there as a start. Best to keep the sickness contained if possible."

Will grabbed the pile and held still while Jonet hefted a few more on top. "Go to the castle with Margery when you're done," he said. "I'll meet you there."

She nodded and turned away to throw clothes of all sizes into a wooden trunk.

"Jonet," Will said, and the serious glint to his voice made her turn. "Don't be late."

• • •

Just as Will left the orphans' home, the warning bell tolled again. He jogged back into the center of the village where families were loading up on mules and horses or heading toward the castle bailey to find space on a wagon. As he looked out at the moor, he saw the first few riders breaching out of the forest. Almost at once a bunched-up group of wagons followed with several men walking, carrying what looked like children. Women surrounded the enclave. They moved slow but steadily toward Druim.

Several ladies screamed when they saw the line of Davidsons. "Calm now," Will said and grabbed up two children as their mother wrapped a baby in a cloth to tie it around her chest. "To the castle. We'll find you a wagon." The woman babbled in Gaelic, her voice edged with panic as she glanced back over her shoulder at the advancing mob.

"Donald!" Will yelled to the warrior he knew. "Tell her to follow me to the bailey." Donald rattled off some Gaelic and grabbed the woman's sack and they all walked briskly forward. Donald called in Gaelic as they moved, even picked up one boy to carry under his arm.

"Everybody out!" Will called for those who could understand him. He looked at Donald. "Do you have enough wagons for all these people?"

Donald shook his head. "We'll load up the young and old, and the others will walk."

"How far is it to Munro Castle?"

"Half a day on horse."

"Then a full on foot," Will said and glanced at the descending sun. "'Twill be a long night."

As they coursed with the flood of people into the bailey, Will glanced around, his height giving him an advantage. No raven curls. He frowned and continued to look as he set the youngsters into a wagon with their mama and her baby. The woman threw an arm around his neck and squeezed.

"She gives ye her blessing," Donald said and set the lad he carried in the wagon.

"Will!" Dory called as she ran to him. "Get Margery, Stephen, and Charissa to the Munros. Searc is a Munro. Remember him?"

Ewan was close by her side, his face grim. Will focused on him. "She'll heal until she's dead. You know that."

"I will not," Dory said.

He bent to her ear. "We all need you. He needs you. Don't kill yourself saving these people."

Will looked to Ewan. The man loved his sister, there was no doubt. He'd keep her as safe as he could. "She'll try to help just one more and—"

"I'll carry her out of here before I let that happen," Ewan said and handed the reins of the horse they'd ridden from the coast to Will.

"Don't let her learn their names." He kissed Dory's head. "Which direction should I head?" he asked Ewan.

"West, stay along the edge of the three mountains."

Will turned. Stephen had the two ponies at the head of their wagon. It was nearly full with children. Who knew Druim held so many wee ones? Stephen waved, his face pinched. Will made his way through the crowd with the nervous horse.

He nodded to Stephen to guide the wagon toward the exit. "Move slowly but keep moving," Will called and led them out of the gates under the pointy portcullis. Ewan would be wise to lower it once the Druim villagers were out. Desperation made even noble people dangerous, and it sounded like the Davidsons were not friends of Clan Macbain.

Will led the horse by the long, leather reins. The wagons had begun to move out of the bailey behind them. Donald road up next to him on a horse. "Where's Jonet?"

Will frowned up at the Druim warrior. "Late." He turned to yell at Stephen. "Follow Donald out of here."

"Charissa?" Stephen said, his eyes wide at the chaos swamping the narrow street.

"I'll get her and Margery. You go."

If anyone thought he looked silly running while towing a trotting horse instead of riding it, no one paid him any attention. The panicked pitch of people on the move melded with the rumble of wagons behind him. As he rounded the corner, following the pebbled road, the moor came into view. "God's bloody teeth," he swore. The Davidsons were approaching the village line. They moved in small groups around each wagon. Faces, drawn and sickly pale, stared ahead, full of desperate determination. This could become lethal quickly. How long had they walked? Sick, frantic, exhausted. Women carrying bundles, children sitting and lying with eyes shut in wagons, men shuffling along, their grip on the wagons as if the lumbering conveyance was holding them from collapsing on the ground. A few horses came alone with riders draped over their necks.

Will had stopped in the street, staring. Donald came behind him, muttering guttural words in his language. Will didn't need the translation to know he was also shocked at the spectacle and the clash that was about to occur.

"Has Caden taken Meg?" Will asked.

"Aye," Donald said.

"Lead the Druim wagons down another route out of here. No one should come any closer to them," Will said. "And Ewan should close the gate. Dory can't handle all this."

Donald rode back the other way, yelling to several other

Druim warriors. "Come on," Will yelled at the horse and started running again toward Jonet's cottage. *Blast!* Which one was hers? He backtracked once in the haphazard little streets. What if she'd gone to the orphans' home?

He could hear the Druim guards yelling warnings to the advancing Davidsons. Weak but hard voices yelled back. Suddenly, Charissa's worry about the Druim warriors shooting the sick didn't sound like a frightened child's nightmare any longer.

"Jonet!" Will yelled as he ran. "Jonet, woman, where are you?" He ran down another side street and paused. There was movement in a house ahead. He ran up to see Charissa jumping up and down as Margery and Jonet threw blankets and pots out into the street.

"What in bloody swiving hell are you doing?" he yelled and grabbed up Charissa. "They are coming. We need to go now!"

"I don't want the illness in my cottage," Jonet said, huffing. She wiped an arm across her damp forehead. "They can use these." She tugged her door shut and slid an iron nail through a latch. It wouldn't deter anyone, but this wasn't the time to argue.

"Get on the horse," Will said. Jonet set her foot in his hands and swung up onto the tall steed. He lifted Margery behind her and Charissa to sit in front of her. The devil's good luck, there was no room for him.

More yelling in Gaelic came from behind him, toward the center of the village. Charissa covered her ears and buried her face in Jonet's chest. Will took off running, pulling the horse behind him, away from the center. He glanced at the sun setting in the west, a perfect guide. He could see a moor up ahead and jogged forward, his other arm pumping at his side.

"Lady Meg!" someone yelled. "Stop! We need yer help!"

A wagon came forward from the moor, nearly blocking their path. "Out of the way!" Will yelled. "This is *not* Lady Meg!"

He didn't slow but dodged the Davidson wagon. Margery screamed as desperate hands reached out toward them. The horse whinnied and kicked up speed. By the devil, he couldn't outrun a horse. He flipped the reins up to Jonet and moved aside so the horse could leap into a run. He ran after them as Jonet spurred the horse forward.

Those on the Davidson wagon turned back to moving into the town. There was little fight left in them, and their hopes still lay on finding help at Druim castle. All along the western edge of Druim, wagons of healthy villagers broke onto the moor. The warriors guided those walking, pulling anyone needing help onto their horses' backs. Will slowed to a jog. Blimey, he'd never seen anything like that in all his wanderings.

He caught sight of Jonet's black head. She'd slowed and turned around, riding back toward him. He shook his head as she pulled up next to him. "You should keep riding."

Jonet looked over Charissa's head back toward Druim. "They aren't going to follow us. They want help, not to infect others."

"Where's Stephen?" Margery asked, and Charissa poked her face up.

"He's safe." Will rubbed the little girl's leg where it hung over the horse's neck. "Driving our wagon with about twenty little ones on board." Will pulled the reins to get the horse moving with him again.

"We can make room," Jonet said.

He shook his head. "I prefer to have two feet solidly under me, and the horse has a long way to go. He'd do better without my weight." They walked across the large, uneven moor and then along a slightly made path through the forest running along the base of the mountains. A few men, with at least one extra person each, rode ahead to help prepare Munro Castle for the influx of Macbains. The sun set, leaving the haphazard caravan in shadows. The moon rose, but thickening clouds raced past it, plunging them in and out of nearly complete darkness. Charissa slept, as did Margery, her head against Jonet's straight back. Whenever he looked up at Jonet, she met his gaze.

"I've never been chased out of a town so quickly before," he said and let his mouth soften into a grin.

She stretched a little in her seat, as well as she could with two sleeping children trusting her to keep them steady. "So ye've been chased out of town?" As a ray of moonlight filtered down, he could just make out her white teeth as she smiled.

"Some of the best," he teased, and she chuckled softly.

"Ye must have some stories to tell," she said.

"I have seen my share of adventure." He paused, and the silence felt heavy so he continued, "There was an island the captain thought was uninhabited. We scoured it to find fresh food, water." She watched him intently as he led them through the trees. "Then we heard the drums."

"Drums?" she whispered.

"Aye, a low beat."

"Let me guess, ye followed the sound rather than

paddling back to yer ship." She shook her head as if the thought was ridiculous.

"Well, certainly." He laughed. "To run from the unknown is foolish. There is enough of the known to run from."

She snorted softly. "And?"

"We came upon a fire in the middle of a dozen or so crude huts. There was a big pot over the fire, and near naked men danced around it."

"Witches?" she asked.

"Nay, cannibals."

Margery gasped behind her, apparently awake. "How did you know they were cannibals?" she asked.

He smiled wickedly as he kept Jonet's gaze, but shook his head. "'Tis not for young girls to hear."

"What did ye do?" Jonet asked.

"Well, now." He chuckled. "They had a good amount of fresh fruit in the trees that we just couldn't leave. We snuck back through the leafy forest, gathering what we could carry. We would have gotten clean away if not for one of their scouts spotting Dory in a tree, plucking a coconut."

"Dory was with you?" Margery asked, her little voice filled with youthful awe.

He laughed. "Aye, she is the best at shimmying up those blasted tall trees."

"Did he chase ye?" a child asked from the wagon that Stephen drove next to them. The lad had steered it closer to them when the forest had given way to another moor. Will turned and saw that he had quite an audience. Ah, his favorite thing. Another boy was speaking in Gaelic to the wagon, perhaps translating.

"The native man, dressed only in skins—"

"Skins of men?" the boy asked.

"Possibly," Will said slowly and heard a little chuckle from Jonet. "But probably from one of the wild cats or boars roaming the forests."

"Did ye see some of the animals?" another asked.

"Shush," the first boy said. "Let him tell the story."

Will continued, "The man had paint on his face, around his eyes to make them seem bigger. He had a spear and tried to throw it up to hit Dory." They all sat in the wagon, eyes as large as he remembered the native's had been when he spotted Dory in the trees above him.

"Dory threw the coconut down on the native."

"Good for her," Margery said.

"But she missed," Will said. This was where his and Dory's retellings always veered apart, but she wasn't out there in the dark with him at the moment. "The native had a blow dart, tinged with poison most likely. He took aim to hit her as she tried to reach another branch. But before he could blow, I lunged into him, knocking him to the leafy ground."

"Ye didn't just slice his head off?" Stephen asked.

"Well now, we were stealing from the man's island." He glanced at Jonet, who watched intently. "That is what pirates do, you know. But he didn't need to lose his life unless he was truly a threat."

"So ye got away then?" the boy in the wagon prompted.

"Not exactly," Will drew out, and the whole wagonload of children stilled to hear the rest. Will continued on in full description of how the native's warning cry had reached the fire, rousing the whole tribe to flush out the crew of the *Queen Siren*. Will had slashed a path through the heavy vines for the crew to follow him back to the beach while dodging blow darts and spears. And he swore he'd heard a wild panther leaping after them also.

The children watched, enraptured, as he performed a few thrusts, demonstrating how they'd been forced to battle for their lives. He with his sword and Dory with her wind had held back the tribe while the crew loaded the dinghy with fruit and themselves.

"We pushed off, still battling a few determined to have our heads and hearts," he said dramatically, grabbing his chest as if to fend off someone from ripping his pumping organ from his rib cage. "And with one last thrust," he slashed his arm through the darkness, making several of the children gasp, "I thwarted the final native. The crew put their backs into the oars, and we rowed to the *Queen Siren*."

They walked in silence for several heartbeats. "Bloody fabulous," the boy said, and Jonet laughed.

"But is it true?" she asked outright.

"Of course," Will said. "On my honor as a pirate."

That made her laugh even harder, but she nodded. "Well, it must be true then."

"Tell us another adventure," Margery insisted.

They had miles to go, and he had enough stories to make the journey seem to go a bit faster. "If you are all brave enough lords and ladies," he warned. Jonet smiled as they all nodded silently. "Very well then." He began a tale about a river trip with lions on one side and angry natives on the other.

Through root-tangled forests and out across two moors, Will continued to conjure exotic beasts and angry natives, leaving out the gruesome facts that would definitely lead to nightmares. Jonet laughed whenever he exaggerated, always sensing when the truth skewed toward the fantastic. The moon continued to plunge into the increasing cloud cover, and a light mist began to fall. Wool blankets came out to cover the wagons. Jonet passed Charissa into Stephen's to hide under cover.

As hours passed, the children in the wagon slumped over into sleep. When the last head bowed, Will let his words trail off. He enjoyed the silence of the night for a while before he felt Jonet brush his arm.

She'd leaned down with a bladder. "Here, ye must be parched from all that talk."

"Like the dirt under the devil's feet," he said and pulled long off the fresh water. He stretched his shoulders. Even with the heat of constant walking, the wet chill slicked against his skin. Just like at sea.

"Let me walk. Ye need a break," she offered.

He was tired. Though he'd spent many nights awake, walking the decks in his turn, he'd never walked the earth so long. But he'd also never make a woman walk in his place. He looked at her to deny the offer, and a flash of moonlight through the trees caught her mutinous expression. She'd recognize a lie as easily as Dory.

"I don't know how to ride a horse," he said softly. "Only been on two all my life."

"I don't believe ye," she said.

He snorted. "You think I would make up something like that. Especially to a woman who was on horseback probably from the cradle."

She studied him, her face softening. "Ye really don't know how to ride?"

"Where would I have learned, living on a ship?"

He walked again in silence onto another blasted moor. The rain tapped down in an annoying beat.

"I'll teach ye," Jonet said. "Ye can show me how to throw the dagger, and I'll teach ye to control a mount."

He glanced at her. The slight haze of moonlight filtered down to glint off her dark hair that pooled thickly around her shoulders to reach her middle back. He nodded. "Aye, 'tis a bargain set."

She smiled, becoming even more beautiful. God's teeth, how he wanted to kiss her again, pull her from that horse and lay her in the sweet, spring flowers in the sunshine, not the cold rain. Everything about Jonet Montgomery was soft on the outside, her velvety voice, her perfectly pale skin, her silky hair. Such a contrast to the strength he sensed on her inside, her cleverness and desire to help the children and even the sick Davidsons with her blankets. And passion, he'd tasted it in her kiss, a tidal wave shorn up by a dike he knew he could crack.

One of the horses toward the muddled front of their army whinnied. The horse carrying Jonet twitched his ears and snorted. She looked out across the moor, and Will heard her breath hitch. He followed her gaze.

All along the edge of the dark forest, sets of eyes glowed back a bright yellow. A quick count brought the number of pairs to twenty or so. "The devil's beasts," he swore as several Druim warriors began to ride toward the front to help the wagon drivers.

"*Madadh-allaidh*!" Will didn't need to ask what the Scotsman had yelled, waking the children and half-asleep drivers. There was no doubt. *Madadh-allaidh* meant wolf.

Chapter Five

Stephen stopped the wagon, and Will held tight to the horse's reins. The skittish animal seemed nervous enough to bolt with the two girls tied to its back. Jonet leaned forward to whisper against the horse's flicking ears.

"And how do you battle against a large pack of wolves?" Will asked, not taking his gaze from the glowing eyes peaking from the dark trees. All the wagons had stopped there on the moor, waiting. The Druim warriors off-loaded their passengers near the wagons and rode to the front of their line.

"With arrows and blades," Jonet said.

"'Tis a good time for you to practice," he said and handed her the black-handled dagger. "Try not to slice anything but a wolf." He pulled his own cutlass and glanced at the children, fully awake and silent in Stephen's wagon. "And now you all will be part of my next tale of adventure." He grinned.

"Move to the center of the wagon," Jonet said, and all the kids climbed close together.

One of the men toward the front whistled long and high. Several others did the same. Was this a battle cry or warning? The line of beasts stepped out onto the moor, their black shapes blending with the low brush, slinking forward. Apparently, the whistle hadn't deterred them.

"I'd rather ye were off the ground," Jonet said, swiveling her head to take in the few wolves advancing from the left.

"I'd rather be on my ship." Will watched the larger animals toward the front. Several smaller wolves dodged back and forth behind them, slinking like shadows just above the moor. They seemed to have their pack strategy perfectly coordinated.

Donald was riding between the wagons, motioning for them to come together. Stephen veered toward the middle, and Will tugged the horse along next to him as he jogged. The damp grasses and mud made the ground treacherous, but he was used to the wet decks of a ship moving beneath him and kept a steady pace. The clouds hid the moon, giving the beasts a chance to slink closer in the dark. He couldn't get a count with their steady shifting.

"Surround the wagons," Donald yelled and repeated it in Gaelic. "All women and children in the middle. No strays."

The children looked petrified. Charissa cried quietly where she sat in the wagon. "Children," Will said. "Remember this moment for it will be a story you'll be able to tell for generations. But you'll have to add some more danger, because this is too easy. Maybe a lion—"

"There are no lions here," the talkative boy from before said.

"Well then, perhaps a dragon," Will countered, his eyes trained on the slinking beasts in the back. 'Twas often the less-obvious dangers that could kill.

A few children giggled. "We don't have dragons, either."

"God's teeth! Scotland seems rather dull," he commented. That got the children talking quietly in the wagon about all the adventures and dangers Scotland had to offer, other than a pack of wolves closing in. Sometimes it helped to think of all the things that weren't about to kill you to remind you that it could be a lot worse.

The horse whinnied and sidestepped, almost knocking into Will. "Blasted animal, keep your path." Within moments, they'd reached the center with the other wagons, the warriors on horses and on foot surrounding them. Will readied his dagger while still holding his cutlass. He could take down at least one with a short blade right between its yellow, demonic eyes. He held it easily in a soft grip, ready to fling it toward the largest. "I'll take out the one in the middle," Will said loudly so Donald could hear.

"I'll back ye up if ye miss," Donald answered.

"I don't miss."

Donald chucked, though it sounded tight. "The beasts have a tendency to dodge."

"Been dodging all my life," Will answered.

Will focused on the leader and felt the prickles on his nape rise as those yellow eyes seemed to focus back. They weren't the soulless, black eyes of a bloodlusting shark, but they were downright eerie.

Donald yelled in Gaelic. Several arrows flew, and a yelp broke through the silence.

"Will!" Jonet called, and he caught sight of one of the

slinkers creeping through the gorse just a few yards out from her horse. Almost at the same time, the large leader lunged forward, breaking into a charge toward them. Will stood ready, his dagger poised.

Off in the woods, a deep howl echoed, and Will caught the glint of steel in a stray beam of moonlight. The leader wolf slowed to trot in a tight circle, his ears pricked high. "What the devil?" Will murmured and watched the wolf pack condense in on itself around the leader as if switching from an offensive strike to a defensive posture. Again, a wolf howl cut through the dark, and movement along the forest line sliced through the shadows. Donald yelled a string of Gaelic.

"What's happening?" Will asked.

"I think we have help," Jonet answered.

"What type of help would stop a pack in mid-attack?"

As if in answer, horses broke through the tree line, but the strangest part was the loping beast running alongside a man onto the field, a smaller shadow following.

"Meg's wolf," Jonet said, "And Searc Munro. Looks like he has a new pet, too."

Will studied the strange trio. He'd met the sixteen-year-old boy, Meg's cousin, in London a month before. As the moon shone down on him, a flash of red reflected in his eyes for the slightest moment. The wolf next to him growled low and loud, and the dog barked a rapid tattoo. Will blinked, and the lad's eyes had returned to shadow. Odd. Maybe it had just been a trick of the night. The wolf pack whined and ran, the leader staying behind to snap at the giant wolf beside Searc before turning to follow his troops back into the forest.

Out of the woods came wagons and more on horseback. "Munros," Jonet whispered

Searc ran forward to meet Donald as did a tall man on horseback with a lady latched on behind him.

"Is anyone hurt?" the lady asked. "Sick?"

"Nay," Donald said, "but there are many back at Druim, the whole Davidson clan."

"Meg is safely at Munro Keep," the lady said. "And she says that another healer is at Druim?"

Donald looked Will's way. "Go," Jonet urged, and he jogged up to the group. The dog ran to him, barking, his tail wagging, and Will recognized the mongrel Searc had befriended in London.

"My sister, Dory, can heal like Meg," Will said and nodded to Searc and his father, Alec. The woman must be Searc's mother, Rachel. "But she can't heal them all, not without dying."

The woman nodded. "I will share the effort with her and teach her how to regain her strength quickly. Alec, let us ride."

"We've brought wagons for your people," Alec said, glancing out at those who had been walking most of the night. "'Tis several more hours to Munro Keep at yer pace. Searc will help guide ye."

Donald sidled close to Alec, and they clasped arms. "Thank ye. 'Tis good to be allies now."

Margery climbed down from Jonet's horse and headed with Searc toward one of the Munro wagons. Women and men without mounts climbed in them as well. Jonet nudged hers close to Will. "'Tis a good time for ye to practice." She grinned down at him, kicked her foot out of the stirrup, and extended her hand. He snorted but took its fragile weight in his own palm and hoisted up behind her in the saddle. Blasted hell, it was a long way to the solid ground.

"Hold on." She laughed and pressed her legs into the animal's sides, making it jump forward and Will to curse. Her perfectly rounded backside rubbed against his groin as they loped across the moor to follow Searc. Devil, how did the men stand it? The heat of her body warmed away the chill from the rain. Her hair slid across his cheeks. The movement of her against him heated his blood to nearly boiling.

"I should ride in front," he grumbled by her ear.

"Ye don't know how to steer a horse."

"I can learn," he gritted out. He leaned into her and inhaled the flower scent she gave off. His breath licked along the rim of her ear. "If I have to continue to grind up against your arse, you won't make it to Munro Keep unravished."

Jonet's spine straightened at his words, but she kept up the rhythmic pace.

"Very well," he said, his fingers fanning out around her middle. "You had your fair warning, woman."

"Blast," she cursed and pulled back on the reins, letting the others continue. They stopped under a tree. The darkness pressed in on them, and she turned in his arms, a slight shiver running through her. "Well, get down and mount in front of me," she said, a bit breathless.

Will stroked her cheek with his thumb, and she caught her breath. "I think I'd prefer to ravish you." He held still, every muscle in his body taut. Would she slap him away, pull back at least, call his mother the whore she probably was? She did none of that but stared back. Perhaps it was his imagination, but her face seemed to move slightly closer into the palm of his hand.

"What?" she whispered. "Without an audience?"

Without sight, his other senses flared high to take in Jonet's sweet essence. He turned her completely in her seat, pulling her soft curves into his hard chest. He tangled his fingers through her fragrant fall of hair to cup her head. He heard her breath as shallow whispers, giving away the racing of her heart. He reeled her in rapidly, remembering the honeyed press from the festival, slanting her mouth to open under his masterful assault.

A soft moan slipped from her, a whisper of the passion he knew boiled under her doe-like skin. The sound shot quick-fire through his veins, turning his well-planned attack into a smoldering kiss with no distinct strategy at all. The world floated away on a sea of sensation. All Will could feel, could think, could taste was Jonet. Her kiss was pure bliss, lush and honest. He felt her heart pounding, her fingers twining in his hair. Never before had he known such power surging through him, yet at the same time drowning him.

He surfaced long enough to make certain she wasn't pulling away. She slid even closer along his body. They breathed against one another, and he trailed heat the length of her jaw to kiss a path down her neck. She murmured something Gaelic that sounded like a request for more. He bent over her, inhaling, reveling in this woman. Blast, he couldn't get enough. He nibbled the softness where her shoulder and neck met, and that little moan welled up out of her again.

The horse shifted under them, and he squeezed his legs to keep steady. Will fell backward along the beast's rump as the devil jumped forward. *Bloody hell!* Jonet screamed, twisting frantically to grab the reins that had slipped from her fingers.

"*Stad*!" she yelled, but the horse continued to prance through the trees.

"Ho there!" Will recognized the voice. He caught his balance and sat upright just as the horse whinnied, pawing its front hooves in the air.

"The devil won't settle down!" Will called.

Jonet pulled back on the reins and patted the horse's neck. "Ye startled him," she said to Searc as he stepped farther out from the trees. The horse whinnied again but calmed under her hand. Will held onto Jonet and the saddle rather than squeezing his legs again. Blasted difficult animal.

"I've never seen a horse shy so from a person," she said and patted at her hair.

"Perhaps he senses Nickum. Meg's wolf is somewhere near," Searc said.

"What are you doing here?" Will asked, a bit surly from being interrupted. "Besides spooking our horse."

Searc frowned in the diffused moonlight. "I noticed ye had stopped." His eyes narrowed at Will. "Wanted to make certain Jonet…and ye were safe out here alone in the dark. Wouldn't want ye to get lost."

Jonet must have picked up on Searc's protective stance. "Searc Munro," she chided. "I'm not some young maid ye need to champion. I can take care of myself."

"There are some things more dangerous than wolves," Searc said slowly.

God's teeth! Apparently, Ewan had talked to the lad about his carousing past. "I know how to behave around a lady," Will said low.

"That's not what Eric Douglas just told me."

"*Och*, Searc," Jonet swore, "the lad is still fuming over my refusing to wed with him. Will and I were just getting to know each other a bit, not that it's any of yer concern."

Searc stood with his arms crossed. *Damn Scot!* Will kicked his leg over the back of the horse and jumped down. He'd rather be on the ground walking than rubbing up against the young widow or falling off a frantic beast. He strode to Searc and heard Jonet clicking to the horse to follow. He met the lad's eyes and again saw a flash of red before it disappeared into shadow. He blinked and spoke softly so Jonet wouldn't be able to hear.

"I don't care what you've heard about me," Will said. "But I will *not* touch any woman who doesn't want me to touch them."

"I never said she didn't want ye to touch her. Just ye should consider what wooing a lass here in the Highlands could mean to her when ye sail away."

The lad was shorter than he and must've known he'd never win a fight, but he stood tall and threatening. Did he hold a soft spot for Jonet?

"Whatever ye are saying, Searc Munro, hold yer tongue," she called and nudged the nervous horse closer. "Now lead the way, or leave us be. I know enough of these woods to figure out the way to yer bloody castle."

Will chuckled. "You heard the lady, lad. Lead the way." The boy turned, and a large, dark shape several yards off to the right slunk along beside them. Sly wolves, overprotective Highlanders, and a spirited lass with kisses that practically robbed him of control. Scotland was certainly less dull than he'd expected.

• • •

Jonet groaned softly, still unwilling to open her eyes. How had her bed gotten so hard? She inhaled, and the faint smell of spice drifted into her. *Will Wyatt.* She blinked and found herself staring at the arched rafters holding up the ceiling of Munro Castle. She pushed onto her elbows to take in the sprawling landscape of sleeping people on the stone floor of the great hall. Several stirred, others were up and moving on silent feet. The fire was low in the hearth, adding a soft glow to the predawn light filtering into the room from high-up window slits. Charissa and Margery slept on one side of Jonet, but the pallet that still held the faint essence of Will was vacant.

Her gaze rested on the wool blanket where his warm body had lain up against her, keeping her cozy through the night. At first it had been nearly impossible to settle down with his bulk surrounding her, but he'd patiently rested beside her, and she'd finally fallen asleep. She glanced around the stirring mass of Macbains. Where was he?

Ann rose across the room and waved to her. Jonet padded delicately between the sleeping people and met her best friend under the arch leading to the back side of the great castle.

"Have you seen Will?" Jonet asked.

Ann smiled. "I saw him lying right up against you all night."

Jonet ignored her blush. "Well, he's not there now."

"I think I saw him headed with the young lad toward the kitchen," Donald said and studied Jonet. "You know he's a pirate," he warned.

Jonet frowned fiercely, taking in both Donald and Ann. "I am a grown woman, no young maid."

"I but want you to be care—"

She held up a hand. "God's teeth, Donald. Will's not even a real pirate. He saves children from slave traders."

"Aye, but he acts like a pirate," Donald said.

"Which may not be altogether bad," Ann giggled, receiving a frown from her brother.

"You stay away from him," Donald ordered, his finger jabbing at Ann.

Ann shrugged. "He seems to be only after Jonet, anyway."

After her? Was he? Well, the kiss certainly seemed to mean that, but was he just after any lass? Could he be tumbling some Munro wench right now?

Jonet turned and headed through the dark corridor. Up ahead was a series of cramped storage rooms. She walked on her toes, afraid to come upon Will kissing some maid, or worse, in one of the dark rooms.

"What are you going to do if you find him back here?" Ann whispered. Jonet dragged her finger across her neck as if slashing a throat. Ann giggled. "The lass or Will?"

"It depends," she whispered back.

"On what?"

"Whoever seems to be enjoying themselves more," Jonet said. The farther she hunted, the angrier she became. Where the blasted hell was he? And with whom? She wouldn't stand to be humiliated again. By the time they reached the walkway to the kitchens, Jonet had talked herself into believing the worst. Will Wyatt was a lecherous scoundrel, pirate or not.

As they passed the kitchen herb garden, Ann plucked off some mint and passed some to Jonet to chew. She chomped on it, and her stomach growled for food. Perhaps the kitchen was a good place to stop. Perhaps Will had actually ended up there. Either way, she and Ann could help with the huge preparations that must be going on to feed the flood of displaced.

The yeasty smell of baking bread permeated the air of the warm room. "*Och*, I'm hungry," Ann said as they rounded the corner. A line of maids stood at the back, seemingly motionless, their eyes riveted toward the great hearths. Some held their cheeks in their palms, one fluttered a hand flat against her heart. The portly chief cook mopped her forehead with her apron skirt.

Ann gasped and tugged on Jonet's sleeve.

"And that is how you make Salamagundi, the heartiest stew found this side of the equator." Jonet stared, her jaw dropping like those around her at the sight of Will stirring a huge, black cauldron over the cook fire. His upper body was completely free of clothing, and his trews fit tightly to his perfectly muscled backside. A fine sheen of sweat along his tanned skin gave him almost a glow in the light of the fire. The faint line of a scar, perhaps a sword slash, crossed over from his shoulder blade down to his hip. The muscles rippled under it as he stirred. Jonet swallowed hard against the sudden dryness of her mouth.

"Let it simmer for a time, and it will be ready with the bread to feed the crowds in the great hall." He shrugged his massive shoulders, and Jonet heard several ladies suck air in quickly. "Now 'twould be better with some turtle meat or fresh fish, but the goose and venison will do. Grapes would also complement the spiced wine." He turned to look at the cook. "Have you any grapes?"

All the cook could do was shake her graying head. Will gave the lady a wicked grin. Well, it probably was just a grin, but everything on that man seemed a wee bit wicked. "Well then, the sweet wine will do."

Will caught sight of Jonet standing with Ann. His smile reached his eyes. "I see you've risen." He nodded to them both. "You can help us get everything passed out." Jonet managed to nod. He sauntered over to her as if she were the only one in the large, hot room. He ran a hand along her hair from the top of her head, down one long tress. "You look a bit tussled." He leaned in and brushed a kiss across her parted lips, as if they were a long-time married couple.

She felt all gazes on her, and Ann made a strangled noise. Will pulled back. "Mmm…mint. I like mint." He turned to head back to the cauldron. Jonet glanced at the awestruck Munro maids, their eyes widening as he stretched his large arms overhead, his fingers catching a wooden rafter to stretch. He must know he was causing a fluster.

Jonet strode over to the fire as the cook yelled for the maids to check the loaves of bread before they burned. "Where is yer shirt?" Jonet whispered tersely next to his shoulder. He nodded toward the corner. "Put it back on."

"I'm hot," he said and gave a cocky grin.

Well, he certainly raised the temperature of every woman in the room. Jonet frowned. "'Tis a common complaint of the kitchen workers, but ye don't see me stripping down indecently."

"I don't mind if you strip down." He winked at her.

She grabbed up his shirt. "Put it back on. Ye can help me bring all this to the great hall. The children will be waking soon and be hungry."

Will clapped his hands together, rubbing them. "My stew will fill them up until supper for certain." He looked so proud of his creation, Jonet couldn't help but smile. He threw his shirt over his head, though it hardly contained all that muscle and man. At least it covered enough to release the women back to their work. God's teeth, he'd have every available lass fluttering around him now. Would they even care that he'd kissed her as if he belonged only to her?

Jonet hesitated. But that was a farce as everyone kept trying to warn her. He didn't belong only to her. Will Wyatt had apparently never belonged entirely to anyone. And she refused to be duped again into thinking that a man could care only for her.

He lifted the heavy cauldron onto a rolling, stone platform made to wheel it into the hall. Several maids volunteered to help take pitchers of ale and cider in, but Cook picked only two. Ann loaded a cart with loaves of aromatic barley bread and wooden bowls, cups, and spoons. They made a parade through the garden and into the main hall. Jonet helped steer the heavy stew as Will pushed it. She saw him pluck some mint and chew it on the way through. Would he want to kiss her again? The thought flipped about in her stomach, and she nearly ran into a barrel inside the door.

"Keep care," Will warned. "If this stew spills, bellies will go hungry."

Granted, the aroma steaming up from the hot contents was curiously tempting, rather like the man who'd created it.

But she hoped he wouldn't be hurt if people didn't appreciate the strange fare. Grapes, of all things? Thank the good Lord Cook didn't have anything so exotic. The different types of meats and spiced wine was strange enough. "I hope the children will like it," she said. "They are not used to pirate stew."

"Ah now, taking a risk to try something new is good for the spirit. Courage must be tested in order to grow in a person." The words were spoken without the usual teasing lilt. She glanced back over her shoulder and met his gaze. His eyes were serious and his voice husky, like when he'd kissed her in the dark forest the night before. He stopped the cart, and she realized she'd nearly run them into the side of the archway that marked the entrance to the great hall.

"Something on your mind, woman?" he asked. "Or are you always so off balance in the morning?"

"I…was just thinking about the children, where they will stay," she covered. "It will be difficult for them sleeping every night on the floor here."

They wheeled the carts in the room that had turned back into a gathering room with tables and benches, the blankets, and pallets stacked along one wall. Jonet spotted the four children she'd been watching at Druim. The oldest girl, Jane, was talking with Margery. They both laughed at something little Charissa said.

"I spoke with Caden and Searc about that this morn," Will said and stopped the pot near the hearth where a cook bar was hanging. "Searc says that the townspeople will take in the children with their mothers, a few per house. The warriors can sleep in the keep or stables, and we'll put the single women above stairs in the empty rooms."

"How about our children?" she asked and then paused. It had rolled off her tongue so naturally. *Their children.* But Will continued to hang the cauldron over the embers.

"Stephen will want to sleep with the warriors, no doubt. I think Margery will take care of Charissa at one of the houses, perhaps with a couple of your charges." He turned and wiped his arm across his forehead with a smile. "That would leave you and me free to sleep where we will."

She opened and closed her mouth twice before she realized that she had absolutely no reply for such a statement. Will chuckled and waved to Ann to bring the bowls over to the hearth. Stephen ran over. "Is that Salamagundi?" The boy sounded like he was already relishing the taste.

"Aye, it is, lad, though without fish or turtle or grapes."

Stephen put his face near the pot and inhaled. "Smells like Salamagundi." He shrugged.

"Salama what?" Margery asked.

"Salamagundi," Stephen said slowly. "The best stew on the seas."

Margery inhaled while Charissa jumped up and down. "Who made it?" Margery asked.

"That would be me," Will answered.

Several warriors came over with the mothers who'd lined up to retrieve some food for their children. Eric laughed. "So the mighty pirate is also a cook maid."

"Aye," Will said. "I'm quite talented at a lot of things." He grinned, and the kitchen maids giggled. Jonet felt herself blush hot. How was it that the man could make a simple statement sound like he was talking about tupping?

Will leaned back against the wall, his feet crossed at the ankles and his muscular arms crossed over his chest. Searc dug right in. He chewed and spooned another scoop into his mouth. Everyone seemed to watch him. Will smiled confidently. Searc began to nod. "Good, really good. The spices are an odd mix, but it's…tasty."

The other warriors started eating as if they hadn't been waiting for the sixteen-year-old to brave a taste first. Jonet made certain that each child was served with a fistful of bread. She ruffled Charissa's curly locks and stood straight, bumping against an unmovable heat. "Oh," she gasped and snapped around.

"You feed everyone but yourself." Will's deep voice slid through her, its timbre kicking her heart into a rapid dance. He held a steaming bowl. "Eat up. You'll need your strength." He winked.

She snatched it from him, nearly sloshing it over the rim. "Everything ye say is…" Her face felt as hot as the soup.

"Aye?" he prodded.

"'Tis said as if ye talked of tupping."

"With you, I am," he whispered back.

"Errr," she huffed and grabbed a piece of bread. She heard him chuckling behind her and joined Ann and the children at the end of one long table. She tasted the stew tentatively, the first touch being strangely flavored. As she let it settle on her tongue, the seasonings wove together into an intricately tasty mix of sweet and salty and exotically spicy. It was good, really good. When she looked up from her bowl, she saw him staring at her, eyebrows raised over his laughing eyes that she knew were a deep, warm brown. She took another spoonful and let her lips turn up in a grin. She nodded.

Will slapped his hands together in one quick explosion

of sound. A maid next to him jumped, a hand going to her bosom. He turned to ladle another helping and strode toward them. He squeezed in next to Jonet.

Ann tilted her bowl to catch the last drop. "It's amazingly good, Will. Where did ye learn to cook?"

"On board the *Queen Siren*. Captain Bart found I had a knack for blending flavors, so I advised the cook and collected ingredients when we were off ship." Jonet felt him shrug, his strong shoulder sliding against her arm. "Nothing will keep a crew working in harmony better than a full gullet and a nice taste on their tongues."

"Same with Highlanders," a maid said with an annoying little titter. The two from the kitchens had followed him over from the hearth. Didn't they have work to do?

Charissa finished her stew and crawled onto Will's lap while she nibbled on her bread.

"All right, little mite," he said. "Stay with Stephen and Margery while I find some clean water. Is there a stream nearby or a place you all go to wash?"

"I'll show ye," one maid volunteered.

"Me also," the other followed quickly.

Jonet turned to look up at him. "Can ye swim then?"

"Quite well," he answered.

"I'd heard that seamen thought it bad luck to learn to swim," she said.

"Foolhardy seamen," he answered. "I bathe everyday off the decks of the *Queen Siren*."

One of the maids looped her arm through his. "We have a fresh water loch just a ways off where ye can bathe."

"Just point me in the right direction."

"Oh, we'll show ye," the simpering girl said and nearly

rubbed up against his arm.

Good Lord, the two would accost him as soon as they had him outside. Jonet stood. "I'd like to see this bathing hole, as well. I need to wash and so will the children, if it's warm enough."

Jonet gave the maids a tight smile, ignoring the glowing one Will cast her way. The pair shrugged and continued to lead Will out the door, Jonet trailing behind them. Caden raised an eyebrow as they trudged past him.

"We are touring the bathing loch," Jonet explained.

"Will and three lasses?" Caden asked, and the maids giggled.

"'Tis a challenging number," Will teased.

Jonet frowned and nearly reached up to shake the two tittering twits.

"Lizzie, Ruth," Searc called, "Cook is looking for ye in the kitchens. She needs help with starting the pies for supper."

The girls deflated. "But we were showing them where to bathe."

"Just Will," Jonet added. "I was going to bathe inside later."

"So ye were just along to watch?" Searc asked her and glanced at Caden.

Jonet felt the blush in her cheeks. "Certainly not to watch." She huffed. "Someone had to protect the innocent," she defended and looked pointedly at the two maids.

"Noble," Will said, "but I've been able to fend off the ladies since I was a lad. And to tell the truth, I'm not all that innocent anymore." He winked. Lizzie and Ruth giggled, and Searc pointed toward the kitchen. Jonet turned to the cluttered table and busied herself stacking empty bowls and cups.

"He's left," Ann whispered. "But he watched ye the whole time until Searc tugged him out the door."

"I don't care," Jonet said in defiance of her own easily swayed heart.

Lizzie and Ruth brought over their cups and the few leftover rolls. Lizzie whispered something in Ruth's ear, making the maid glance at Jonet. "Och now, I don't think we need worry. Will Wyatt needs a lass who will keep him entertained." She gave Jonet a look that clearly showed she didn't think Jonet was up to the task.

Jonet's indignant fury dissolved under the maid's pitying look. Ann took a step toward the cart with a bowl and stumbled, sending cold stew flying forward to slop all over Ruth.

"Pish!" the girl yelled as Lizzie gasped. Ann tossed the bowl on the cart.

"So sorry," Ann said and held her hands to her cheeks in feigned shock.

Ruth growled, shooting her evilest look at Ann, and stormed away. Lizzie wheeled the full cart after her. When they rounded the corner, Ann turned to Jonet.

"I don't think he would have done anything with those fools. Men like the attention, like bairns."

"Well, if he thinks I am one of those maids he can love for a night and walk off, then he's mistaken," Jonet said.

"Surely he's smart enough to know that," Ann said. She leaned into Jonet. "That will be yer way of knowing if he's really sweet on ye. If he stays away from the rest of the lasses, then ye know he's waiting for ye."

"Aye, but what if he waits for me and *then* goes after the other lasses?"

A memory of her husband from years ago surfaced in her mind. He'd been kind to her, but she'd been young, scared, and rather shy in her new home far away from her clan. After their very awkward wedding night, she'd caught him kissing a more experienced maid at Druim. The more time he spent with other lasses, the more pitying looks Jonet got from the villagers. It soon became obvious that Machar only came to her bed to try to get her with child, which didn't happen before he was killed.

As she'd grown and distanced herself from the stigma of being undesirable, she'd relaxed, made her own friends. But she'd never again been intimate with anyone, preferring instead to flirt and maybe try a kiss with Ewan, nothing that would make her vulnerable. And she definitely didn't need a swarthy pirate showing everyone that she wasn't worth more than a quick tumble.

Jonet shook her head at her friend. "Nay, Will Wyatt can do whatever he likes. I care naught."

Chapter Six

Jonet kept to her word, at least on the outside. She'd busied herself making certain the children and adults of Druim were as comfortable as possible during their exile. Food was rationed, though the warriors brought in fresh meat almost daily from the surrounding forests. Will had been quite creative in the kitchens working with whatever he was given. It was amazing what flavorful creations came from so little. Jonet could only imagine the flirting going on with Lizzie and Ruth, so she kept well away.

Meg and Caden, along with Searc, kept both clans running smoothly while Alec and Rachel were away with the Davidsons quarantined at Druim. A rider from Druim came on the fifth day to let Caden know that Dory and Rachel were working together to help the most serious and that although things were still grim, they felt the majority would be healed. But it would take a fortnight at least. Fiona, Rachel's best friend, and the elderly Druim housekeeper,

Evelyn, returned with the rider with a wagon full of herbs, blankets, and baked breads.

Jonet stepped silently to the door of the small bedroom she shared with Ann above the great hall. It was before dawn, but she hadn't been able to fall back to sleep after the dream she'd had, a dream of laughing brown eyes and a burning touch. Her face still flushed over the achy sensations that had awoken in her, sensations she'd never experienced before. She'd successfully avoided Will during her waking, but at night the blasted devil snuck into her mind.

She slipped through into the dark hall and turned to close the solid oak door. She stopped, her gaze riveted to the protruding blade in the center of the door. A scrap of parchment curled up from the piercing blade. She held the glow of her thin candle so she could read the slanted script.

Time for lessons.

She yanked the *sghian dubh* from the door and whispered a curse. The stubborn man still thought she was helpless. She set it inside the door on the floor and continued to the stairs. When had Will stuck it there? She hadn't heard anything. Aye, she was too busy rolling around with the pirate in her dreams.

In the great hall, Druim warriors slept on scattered pallets. Some were already up. Luckily, Will seemed absent, probably half-undressed in the kitchens. Jonet strode across the bailey toward the stables. Perhaps she would go for a short ride along the edge of the village before the children came looking for her. She needed time to collect herself after the fitful night.

The barn was quiet, just the swishing of horse tails and

the scurry of mice fleeing Searc's numerous cats. A crunching sound and a deep murmur came from a stall near the end. Jonet froze.

"There now, an early apple for you this morn. Mayhaps you'll keep me on your back today." Will stood in the soft glow of a lantern, rubbing his hand down the horse's long nose as it munched. The beast tossed his head as if to nod, and Will chuckled.

Jonet's chest burned with the need to inhale. She turned and cringed at the sound of her skirts brushing the straw scattered on the dirt.

"You didn't strike me as a woman who ran away." His voice, so like the voice whispering in her ear from the dream, sent a tingle down her back. But the tone was different, disappointed. He stood still and silent, as if waiting with her to see what she would do.

She should continue out of the barn, put as much distance between them as she could. But the thought of him thinking her a coward made her turn back instead. "There is a huge difference between running away and refusing to be made a fool of."

Will leaned back against the wall, his arms crossed over his broad chest. The dawning light filtered into the stable, reflecting a scowl on his face. "So talking to me makes you a fool?"

"No," she said and crossed her own arms. "But kissing ye does, and every time ye get close enough to talk to me," she paused to huff, "ye kiss me."

"You don't seem to mind."

"Not when we're in the middle of it." She flapped a hand. "But afterward, when it's obvious to everyone that ye kiss a lot of lasses. I won't be made a fool of, Will Wyatt, and I won't be one of yer simpering, giggling, tupping lasses."

He took a step closer, and she steeled herself not to retreat. She wasn't an idiot, damn it, and she wasn't a coward. If she could just stop her heart from flying as he approached like a giant cat stalking a mouse. "So people say I've been swiving with the maids here?"

She frowned at him. "No, not yet anyway, but it's just a matter of time. They fall all over ye, and ye encourage it." She tapped her foot on the hay, thinking about Ruth and Lizzie from the kitchens. "Even yer own sister warned me that ye'd never been loyal to one woman."

He stopped, his features turning even darker, making Jonet go over what Dory had said at Druim. The lethal look on his face made her worry over what Ewan's new wife would have to deal with when Will met up with her again.

"And Searc warned me, too," she added.

His eyebrow shot up. "What exactly left the lad's tongue?"

"Well, it was more of a look, like I was stupid to follow after ye."

"I don't want you to follow after me," he said slowly, as if he was trying to let his anger soften but having a hard time of it.

Jonet swallowed. "Ye don't?"

He shook his head. "I want you to walk next to me." He took another step toward her. She kept her arms crossed like it might keep him away. Will scrunched up his very talented mouth for a moment. He shook his head. "Those other girls don't mean anything. They're just giggly children."

"Ye seem to like them," she countered.

He grinned a lopsided smile. "I've always liked an audience to appreciate my antics. The more laughing the better. It doesn't mean I want to pounce on them."

Oh, he wasn't softening her up that easily. "So ye haven't kissed anyone here?"

"Aye I have," he said slowly, "and it was so hot I nearly boiled on the spot."

Jonet couldn't quite catch her breath when he looked at her like that. "Ye mean…"

"I suppose it wasn't really here," he said and took another step closer. "It was on that dammed, tall horse on the way here." He stood before her and let his large hands rest on her shoulders. "I wonder if the stables will ignite when I kiss her again."

Her arms suddenly down, Jonet felt the heat of his body as he enfolded her against him. Could he feel the pounding of her heart? As Will's lips met hers, Jonet felt her stiffness at his touch melt until she could have been a puddle at his feet. But he held her to him, not letting her fall or escape the onslaught of liquid fire tearing through her muscles, making her limp yet full of frenzied power at the same time. Those same arms that she'd used to block his advance now wrapped around him, her fingers tangling in his soft waves of brown hair.

Will growled low in the back of his throat, and Jonet answered with her own as she opened her mouth and tilted her face knowing…wanting…insisting he follow. And he did, tasting her, loving her mouth. Mint and clean man filled her, boiling her blood.

She flattened her hands down his back, running the lines of muscles to the top of his low-slung trews. She felt his fingers gliding in her hair, tugging out the two pins she'd put in to hold the mass out of her face. His palm cupped her cheek, a thumb teasing circles, while his other hand held her against him. She felt his hard body all along her softness, the contrast so immense that she felt dizzy. She tugged and crept under the edge of his linen shirt to the heat of his bare skin. *Och!* So hot. What would it feel like to be naked against his skin? Surely she'd burn.

With a swift tug, the heat was gone, leaving ice so stark she gasped. Will had spun them, tucking her behind him as he stood before the open stable door, blade in hand. She grabbed hold of the edge of his shirt to keep from falling.

"Bloody hell, Jonet!" Her still-pounding heart dropped into her stomach. Eric. She took a full breath and tucked her hair behind her burning ears before stepping up beside Will.

"You look tupped!" he yelled, a sneer on his face as he eyed Will. "He's just sating his lust with you, don't you see that? He'll lie that he loves you, and then he'll leave you after he gets what he wants. You should know better."

Jonet's breath hitched in her throat. Was that what people would say? That she should know a cheating man when she saw one, that she was a fool for falling for lies again?

"What are you saying?" Will demanded, and Jonet realized Eric spoke in Gaelic.

"'Tis none of yer concern, pirate."

"Jonet is my concern." Will looked down at her and put his arm around her stiff shoulders. "And whatever you just said," he looked straight at Eric, "is about to get your throat slit."

"Nay," Jonet managed and grabbed Will's throwing arm.

Face flushed and mind nothing but mush, she couldn't think of anything else to say.

Eric looked back at her, a look of genuine concern softening the disgust she'd seen there. He spoke in English. "He's just like Machar."

She stiffened, and it was as if a curling wisp of smoke exploded into a bonfire next to her. In the fastest lunge she'd ever seen, Will leaped forward, thrusting Eric against the wall next to the stable door. His palm spanned Eric's throat, cutting off the man's airway. Eric stood on his toes to keep from hanging.

It happened in what seemed like a heartbeat, but before she could move, Caden and Searc ran into the barn. "Bloody hell, Will, let him down," Caden ordered.

"Who is Machar?" Will said, the words seeping out of his clenched teeth. Eric's eyes bulged from his head. "Who am I being compared to?"

Caden glanced at Jonet, and she blinked back the moisture there. It had been such a terrible time in her life, full of pity and embarrassment. A young, thin lass that couldn't keep her husband warm. Caden had been barely a man, but he'd known all about her disgrace. Yet he didn't say anything. Of course not. It was her history to share if she wished.

"Caden," Searc warned, watching Eric's face turn reddish purple, but Caden held up his hand.

Jonet stepped forward but didn't touch Will. "He was my husband."

At her words, Will released Eric, letting him slide abruptly to the ground, gasping. Will stepped back, but Jonet stared at Eric floundering in the dirt. She clasped her hands together.

Caden and Searc hauled Eric up. "Serves ye right for meddling where ye've been told ye're not welcome," Caden rebuked loudly for the half-dozen warriors now standing outside the stable doors to hear.

"Ye're lucky he didn't gut ye," Searc joined in. "A pirate will gut a man for looking wrong at him."

Donald stood braced by the door and shook his head at Eric, his glance at Jonet grim. "Yer innards could be all over the ground for saying foolhardy lies, lad."

Lies? Were they really lies? Jonet stood there, numb, while the other warriors became scarce after Caden and Searc dragged Eric away. Her feet felt stuck. Will stood apart, but his presence was so immense that she inhaled shallow breaths as if there wasn't enough air.

"Are you all right?" he said softly.

"I need to go," she whispered but still couldn't move. He did instead. He moved to stand before her again, close but not touching.

She stared at the ground between their feet, her toes on the edge of her skirts, his boots large like the man. For a long moment, he didn't move, didn't say anything. She concentrated on breathing and not letting the old childhood tears roll out.

"So…" he started. "You were wed to a large, handsome devil of a man." There was a casual grin in his voice as if he was trying to lighten the mood. "He must have loved you—"

Jonet snapped her eyes up to his. "No, he didn't. He didn't love anyone but himself."

"Did he hurt you?" Will asked low, his mood switching from light to lethal.

Her eyes did water then. She couldn't hold her tears anymore, but she refused to acknowledge them.

Will looked up at the ceiling, his hands in fists. "Swiving bastard of a whore's pig. He'll suffer the day I find him in hell."

"Nay." She shook her head. "He didn't beat me. He hardly did anything to me." She wanted him to understand. Maybe then he'd realize that she wasn't the woman for him, a woman who could keep a man like Will Wyatt interested past simple flirting. She met his gaze. "He ignored me."

"Jonet!" Ann's voice came from the bailey. "Jonet, we need ye!"

Jonet's feet finally released, and she brushed past Will out of the stables. Ann ran up and grabbed her arm. "It's the bairn. Meg says 'tis coming."

• • •

The babe was on the way. Women ran hither and thither throughout the keep fetching linens and rope and herbs. Twice Will hauled up cauldrons of water to the door of the room Caden and Meg had been staying in.

"Blasted women's work," Caden muttered at the door. "Won't let me in."

"Meg would know if something was wrong," Will reminded him. "Dory always knew when she was catching the ague before it showed up." He patted Caden's back and headed down below. The corridor was too closed in, and the soon-to-be papa's nervous energy would surely drive Will crazy. He'd tried to ask Caden about Jonet's last comment, but the man could only focus on the muffled cries from inside the chamber.

Donald stood at the bottom of the stone steps. "You better go up to him," Will said. "He needs someone besides the door to growl at." Donald nodded but didn't look too happy to replace Will.

Will strode outdoors toward the sparring field where Druim and Munro warriors trained. A group of boys fought a mock battle with wooden swords. Younger children chased spring butterflies and picked flowers in the fields. Margery and Jane waved to him. Very helpful girls. He walked toward the men who trained with long swords. His own sword was a cutlass and curved for close quarters fighting. On board a ship, the Scottish long swords would be more of a hindrance than a help.

"Damn devil," Will swore and stopped, his hands curling around the hilt of his cutlass. Eric stood amongst the younger men. The sight of the lad shot lightning through Will. What the hell did the fool mean, he was just like Jonet's dead husband? If the man ignored her, he was either an idiot, completely blind, or preferred men. And nothing like Will, who, no matter how he tried, couldn't ignore her.

Searc walked up. "I'd be thinking ye'd be anxious to go down there and beat some sense into Eric."

"If I start, I might not stop at a beating, and then you all would try to kill me, and more of your men would die. All around a bad omen for the birth of Caden's babe."

Searc chuckled. "Prudent of ye."

Will turned to the boy, who was fast growing into a man. He frowned. "You think I'm not good enough for her."

Searc thought for a long moment. "I suppose in all honesty, I don't really know ye, but I know Jonet, and she's…a really good person." He looked at Will. "So no, I don't think ye are good enough for her."

It was honest. Will nodded. "I'm no saint." *Hell.* He wasn't good enough for a woman like Jonet Montgomery. He'd heard from an early age that he was good for nothing and no one; that was until Captain Bart had rescued him and taken him as his own son.

"None of us are saints," Searc replied and shrugged. "But a man who purposely hurts a sweet lass like Jonet will suffer." The silence stretched for a long moment. "Well, I'm headed down if ye'd like to come. Ye're welcome, but ye can't kill Eric."

"Did you hear what he said to Jonet in the stables?"

Searc nodded.

"I don't know Gaelic, and I have no idea how I could be like her foolish, dead husband who ignored her."

"Is that what she said?"

"Aye, but I don't know what it means."

"It's for her to explain if she wants." Searc walked away.

Will cursed. He wanted answers and he was tired of the warnings. Normally, he'd stay well away from a complicated wench like Jonet. There'd never been one before that plagued his mind. But the green-eyed Highland lass was bewitching.

• • •

He didn't see Jonet nor hardly any of the women of the keep until the next morning. A cluster of grinning, sweaty women came down the steps, causing all the waiting men and children to rise. Jonet stood in the front. Her eyes met his, and the joy he saw there melted the knot in his gut.

"'Tis a healthy boy," she called out, and the room erupted in cheers. She looked away as a number of people came forward with questions.

One of Caden's advisors, Old Kenneth, elbowed Angus next to him. "The old Macbain would rise from his grave if he knew his grandson had just been birthed in Alec Munro's bed." He chuckled and raised his ale in salute. "'Tis a new world."

"That it is," Bruce agreed and belched loudly.

"We will have the blessing and a celebration this evening!" Ann called from a chair she'd climbed upon to be heard. Another round of cheering broke out. "But now we're headed to sleep," she finished.

Will followed Jonet with his gaze. Twice she noticed but looked away rapidly, a little stain of pink in her cheeks. She stayed below just long enough to grab some food. Will watched the gentle sway of her skirts as she climbed back up the stairs.

Donald stopped by him. "Come hunt with us today for the feast tonight."

"Do you have a bow I can borrow?"

"So ye know how to work one of those?" Donald laughed.

"I can shoot a gull flying twenty yards up and harpoon a thrashing shark."

"Well now," Donald slapped his back, "let's see ye prove that boast."

Will spent the rest of the day riding and hunting with the Druim and Munro warriors. Donald and Searc seemed vigilant on keeping him well away from Eric, who cast sideways sneers whenever he could. Will's fingers had bruised the idiot's neck, but he'd recover. The lucky bastard.

By the end of the day, he'd named the horse Ewan had given him after his captain and adopted father, Bart, both of them being headstrong and belligerent, and decided to keep the spirited beast. After all, Ewan had Gaoth. The steed had refused to move when a wild boar charged him, as if he could block the crazed beast after Will had jumped down to spear him. The fool animal would have been run through if Will hadn't hit the boar right between its black eyes. Aye, stubborn as his father.

"Good hunting," Donald said and nodded toward the hares tied to Bart's saddle. The boar was dragged behind.

Will smiled. "These Highlands aren't as dull as I'd imagined." Donald and a few others laughed.

"And the lasses are the best in the world," Gavin said. "Ye've seen lasses of the world. What do ye think?"

He could see the trap and smiled. "Ah now, I've met quite a few beauties." He inhaled fully. "But I must say, Highland lasses smell the sweetest." Half the men laughed immediately with the rest following after Gavin gave a quick translation.

"Jonet smells sweet," Donald said and watched him carefully.

"Now, where I come from, a man doesn't sniff and tell." He met Donald's piercing stare. Either he was sweet on Jonet himself, or the lanky man felt it his duty to be a big brother to her as well as Ann. Or as Searc had warned, all the Highlanders were watching out for Jonet. After a moment, Donald nodded.

At Munro castle, Will carried the huge beast to the kitchens and headed to the small lake for a swim. Was Jonet still asleep somewhere in the castle? What did she look like when she slept? That first morning at Munro Keep, he'd been jarred awake by one of the children crying on the other side of the room. He hadn't had time to watch her slumbering before another woman needed his help finding the kitchens. Before he knew it, he'd been enticed to make his stew.

Did she make little mewing sounds or possibly snore? The thought made him smile. He hoped that she snored. She'd be utterly indignant when he told her.

He worked the soap that the cook had given him through his hair and over his body. What if he never got the chance again to see Jonet sleep? The thought bored into his chest, causing an ache. He stretched in the icy mountain water with each cutting stroke. Riding all day used different muscles than climbing masts and fighting. Soon the burn of exertion drove off the cold and his melancholy thought.

Of course he would get another chance. Will Wyatt didn't give up. But then, what if she did want more? He didn't want to hurt her, and he was definitely a scoundrel, although no other woman in all the world had caught his attention for so long, despite their open invitations. Hell, never before had he spared so much thought on a woman. He cut across the lake, pushing the churning thoughts from his mind.

The great hall was strewn with fresh rushes. Spring flowers swooped, linked together in garlands, along the stone walls. The minstrels from Druim were set up in the corner. Humphrey waved to him and pointed to his drum. Will chuckled and nodded. He'd take over the faster-paced rhythms.

The room was filling with villagers, some he recognized from Druim, and others he assumed were Munros. Both sides wanted to see the child possessed both Munro and Macbain blood. Their union and this child tied the two warring clans together in peace, ending the century-old war.

Will grabbed an ale and waited with Searc for the women and the babe to come downstairs. Ann stepped down first and waved her arms, bringing the crowd to an excited silence. Behind her came Jonet, followed by Meg in Caden's arms, the new mother holding a small bundle to her chest.

The crowd cheered. Jonet smiled out at everyone, her face radiant. The dark circles under her eyes from earlier had faded. Good, she'd slept. Ribbons of blue slid along her dark curls. They matched the blue in her gown, cinched tightly at the waist and cut low enough to show the lace top of her chemise. Her gaze washed about the room, and he straightened. She turned her head, her eyes finding his face, and stopped. He nodded slightly to her, and a little grin softened her mouth as if she was truly happy to see him.

"Ah, woman," he murmured. "Your heart is hard to hide." It both warmed him and tightened his gut.

The blessing of the priest happened quickly. Caden stood so proud with his son, whom they named Kincaid after his mother's family. Will walked up with Searc to spy the wee babe who slept through all the ruckus.

"My mother's blood runs in the bairn," Searc said and studied the little thing. "As does yours, Meg. Does he have a dragonfly birthmark?"

Will knew that Dory had such a mark. Perhaps all healers did.

"The dragonfly only runs through the women's line," Meg answered.

"But does he have any mark?" Searc pushed and touched

the child's wrinkled knuckles. "Perhaps with so much magic on both sides, he's been born with some."

"I haven't seen him glow at all," Caden said and smiled at his son. "Though he seems rather busy with sleeping and suckling."

"He's a handsome babe," Will complimented as Searc moved off. "And I've seen my share of babes, though none quite this fresh."

Meg seemed to study him for a moment, a knowing smile on her lips. "Every time I bring up your name, Will, her heart races," she said softly.

He stood there watching the babe's little fingers wrap around his own.

"It became a game through my labor," Meg continued. "Jonet held me. Whenever I mentioned you, her heart would speed up, and her cheeks would pinken. She has strong feelings for you."

"Meg," Caden drew out, as if warning her, but she didn't seem to care.

"Those strong feelings might not be good ones," Will pointed out.

She smiled. "Oh, I think they aren't too bad. But you need to talk to her. Don't ignore her."

Ignore? The word resonated in Will, and he glanced around the room until he saw that cascade of dark tresses. She laughed at something Donald was saying. Absolutely breathtaking. Her husband had ignored her. It was just another word for not loving her. Will bowed to the happy new parents.

He stepped up to the small circle, and Donald switched to English. "Here he is, and as ye can see, quite whole despite trying to protect his horse from a charging boar."

"Bloody Bart wouldn't get out of the way," Will said.

"Bart?" Jonet asked.

"I named our horse Bart after my father, Captain Bartholomew Wyatt."

"I thought he was my horse," Jonet said.

"You didn't name him, so I thought he was without a master." He winked at her.

"He even knows how to sit him now," Donald chimed in.

"Bart will do practically anything for green apples," Will said. "Except step out of the way of a charging boar." They all chuckled, and Jonet smiled, a bit of her saucy ease returning. It was a start. The small victory warmed his middle. He leaned against the wall and watched her talk, her pink lips moving. God's teeth, how he wanted to kiss them again, but he had to be patient. Wooing Jonet was the biggest challenge he'd ever undertaken before. That must be the reason each smile won from her made him feel like cheering.

Charissa ran toward him, Stephen trailing behind. He scooped her up in a hug. "Can we go?" she asked.

"Where, little one?"

"They are building a fire in the bailey and moving part of the celebration out there. I think the children are running amok in here," Stephen said as if he was quite the adult.

"Of course, but don't go out of the castle walls," Will said and kissed her soundly on the head before depositing her back down.

Jonet took a step closer and brushed at his shirt. "Ye have tart crumbs all over ye now." Her fingers whispered along his skin, but the result shot hot through him. Blast, he'd embarrass himself if he didn't get control. He'd have to start wearing the Highland skirts soon.

"Thank you," he murmured and grabbed her hand to tuck it into his arm and started walking. "Why don't we see what the children are up to outside."

Jonet continued beside him with Ann and Donald following. It felt good to have her there. A fire in a stone circle sat off to one side with children poking branches into it. The sun sank lower, and the flames cast dancing shadows on the bailey wall. Breads, rabbit pies, and cups of ale and cider circulated. The pork would need to cook longer, but more than one villager congratulated Will on the prize. Several benches ringed the fire pit, and they sat.

"I just might have an idea for a meal with the leftover pork," Will said and grabbed a discarded stick. He drew a rough rendition of a boar. "Do you happen to have apricots this far north?"

"Nay," Donald answered.

Will shrugged. "Maybe Cook has some apples I can use."

"Whatever makes ye think to use fruit with meat?" Ann asked.

Will smiled at the young woman. "I like to play with foods, mix them into interesting combinations. A bored crew leads to trouble. I make certain they aren't bored."

"Yer captain must be having a hard time while ye're away," Jonet said and grabbed a stick herself.

"Well now, Captain Bart can handle his men, he did so before he found me. I just make myself useful."

"He found ye?" Jonet asked. Will noticed the avid attention from the other two as well.

"Aye, in the hull of a slave ship headed to Asia. He was saving the children on board. I was one of them."

"Do ye remember yer life before that?" Jonet asked.

Did he? He'd always blocked it out. He shook his head. "Not much." He looked directly at Jonet. "Just a hazy feeling of being ignored."

He didn't look down, even though the feeling would have pushed him that way. Aye, he knew that feeling of being ignored, but for him, it was better than being under the cruel eye of a slave trader or harsh master. What did it mean for Jonet?

Charissa plopped into his lap. The boar's tail was brought out to roast over the fire, and Will gave pieces to all the children, much to their delight. The day gave way to night as they ate and chatted. The children ran in a game of tag, and a light session of gameball got the kinks out of Will's legs from riding.

He watched Jonet and Ann walk back in through the bailey gate, having taken the children safely to their temporary beds in the village. As the evening wore on, more whisky flowed, and the jokes became bawdier. Will relaxed by the fire while watching Jonet out of his periphery near the castle steps. She laughed with Ann, who handed her a flask. So, the woman imbibed a bit. Maybe the whisky would loosen her tongue. He saw her look his way, and he met her gaze with a smile and nod.

Jonet took the flask and walked over, sitting on the bench beside him but not touching.

"The children in their beds?" he asked casually.

"Tucked in tight and tired."

"Are you tired?" he asked, not sure where he should try to take the conversation. Confound it. His stomach was tight like a nervous lad's.

She shook her head. "Would ye like a sip? 'Tis good Scot's whisky."

His finger brushed hers as he took the offering. The fire slid easily down his throat. "Oooh, 'tis good."

"Be careful, 'tis potent stuff," she warned.

His eyebrows rose. "I'll do that." Though he doubted any sip of spirits could affect him much. Drinking was a regular competition with the crew. He could certainly hold his liquor.

"So what do ye do on that ship to pass the time? Ye mentioned cooking strange concoctions, and ye play the drums and, of course, keep the ship working."

"There's always something to do," he said and crossed his legs at the ankles before the fire. He glanced at her and grinned. "We have contests."

"Contests?"

"Aye, drinking, throwing the dagger, dancing, even poetry."

She laughed. "I can't see a bunch of pirates sitting on deck reciting poetry."

He chuckled with her. "Well now, 'tis not the type of poetry ye would hear in a gentlewoman's parlor."

"Oh?" She took another sip of the whisky, her little mouth closing on the swallow. "What type of poetry do pirates recite?"

"The scandalous kind," he whispered against her ear.

She turned to him. "Give me an example." She raised one eyebrow as if daring him.

He grinned up at the stars overhead, his mind quickly fastening on a rhyme. "The competition lies in coming up with something that makes sense, rhymes, and is terribly shocking."

She snapped her fingers a couple times. "Very well, let's see ye come up with something fresh and new.

He nodded, looked at her, his grin wicked, and began.

"There once was a girl from Madrid,

Who married a dandified prig,

So at night she would creep

To her bloke down the street

Who loved her clean out of her wig."

She stared at him, her lips parting for a moment until a frown emerged.

"I know, 'tis rough," he said.

She took another little sip. "It didn't shock me. I just don't like the subject matter."

"Oh, how about this then.

There once was a lass from Druim

Who had breasts as pale as the moon.

With midnight-black curls

And blue eyes with green swirls

I'd gift her my heart in a spoon."

Jonet's frown melted rapidly with her laughter. "In a spoon? Ye wouldn't win the contest with that one."

"And it wasn't nearly shocking enough," he agreed.

"Green swirls?" she asked and blinked.

He stared into her eyes. "Well, 'tis more like little rays of sun, but swirls rhymed with curls."

She had moved closer, within easy reach of a kiss, but he waited. She was skittish after the incident in the barn. "Beautiful, midnight curls around emerald eyes," he said low, letting his compliment sink in. Her lips were perfect and soft and would taste like Jonet and pure Scot's whisky, free and untamed.

She blinked and straightened back as if catching herself. *Blast!* She glanced around and settled back on her bench. Will hid his frustration in a relaxed smile and took a swallow of the burning liquid.

"Here's one that will completely shock you," he boasted, trying to recapture the lightheartedness that seemed to be slipping.

"Ye might find shocking me harder than ye imagine."

"Ah now, something wicked." He glanced at the heavens again as he spun together another quick ditty.

"There once was a girl in a book
Who swung from a rope on a hook.
With her legs open wide
So her lover could slide
In and out, in and out, 'til she shook."

Jonet choked a bit on her laugh, her hand against her lips. "Quite scandalous," she said. "And quite ridiculous."

He laughed with her, thankful she wasn't prudish. Aye, they would get along fine. "What is ridiculous?"

"A rope and hook, like we used to hoist Meg up to help the birth." She shook her head.

"I believe," he said and took up the stick to scratch a scene that had caught his eye from a book his father's favorite whore had, "that the ropes hold the woman's ankles and back so she hovers over the bed…"

Jonet stopped laughing and stared between him and the drawing. "Impossible." She grabbed the flask from his other hand and took a bigger drink. "Have ye…?" She pointed to the picture.

"Nay, but I've seen it in a book."

"A book? What the hell kind of book would have that in it?"

Will rubbed the picture away with his boot. "One from the Far East. Adela, my father's friend, she runs a brothel. She traded for it."

"A book with drawings like that?"

He grinned wickedly. "Lots of drawings showing what a man and his lady can do to one another in privacy."

"Tupping?"

He nodded.

"There is more than one way?" she asked softly.

He stopped the chuckle in his throat. She was serious, and he surely wasn't going to make her feel stupid for her lack of sexual prowess. Quite the opposite. The fact that there had been no others showing her the many ways of feeling pleasure, that it could be him alone, warmed him. He laid his big paw over her hand. "Aye, Jonet, there are many ways, and the fact that you don't know any but one," he smiled, "makes you—"

"Ignorant," she finished and glanced away, though she didn't tug back her hand.

"Nay." He caught her chin with one finger and prodded her gaze to his. "Fresh and utterly enticing."

She blinked twice and leaned in. The kiss was tentative and too brief. She sat back. "Show me another picture." She glanced down at the ground. "One ye prefer." Her eyes opened wide. "Actually nay, I don't want to know what ye've done." She flapped her hand. "Just what ye think is interesting."

Thank the good Lord. He certainly didn't want to go into his past exploits with women who were nothing like his pure

Highland lass. Suddenly, the thought of his past debauchery hurt his head and tightened his shoulders. He rubbed his hands over his face.

"Come now." Jonet nudged him. "Something else must have stood out to ye."

He nodded and chuckled, picking up the stick again. He glanced around, but the children were all to bed and most of the adults were wandering off for the night. "Here's one," he said and slashed the ground with quick strokes. He lowered his voice. "So the lady kneels and leans on her hands while the gentleman comes behind her over her back."

"That works?" she whispered.

"Aye," he said and he stopped himself from giving his opinion of just how well it worked. He rubbed his boot over the dirt and started fresh with another. "Here's one where the lady lies on her back with her feet up here."

She stared intently while he drew several other positions ending with one with the woman kneeling on the bed and the bloke standing behind her. She leaned against his other arm as he drew and studied the quick diagrams. He froze when he felt her breath on his ear.

"Ann said that one of the maids at Druim put her mouth here on a man," she whispered, moving his stick. She looked at him, her face so close. She blinked, and he could hardly breathe. He forced an inhale, and a grin melted across his face. "I hope the bloke knew enough to return the favor by putting his mouth here," he said and moved the stick back to the woman.

She turned back to stare down at the end of his stick. "Really?" She studied him. "And ye do that to a woman?"

He leaned forward and kissed her gently. "How about

you don't ask me about what I've done with other ladies, and I won't ask you about your past sins with Ewan Brody."

Jonet sat up straight, her brows drawn until they relaxed with a little laugh. "Ye think I've lain with Ewan?"

Will's stomach knotted tight. He surely didn't want to think about Jonet with anyone, but especially the dashing Highlander that his sister had fallen for. "I've learned not to ask a question when I don't wish to be burdened with the answer. You should consider that before you ask." He nodded to emphasize his point.

Jonet laughed, her eyes sparkling with the firelight. "'Tis a bargain." She nodded, but continued quickly. "But I've never slept with Ewan. A few kisses, perhaps."

Will watched her. She didn't look like she was lying, and she'd have no need to. The knot in his gut began to melt away. "Well then, that's the best news I've heard since stepping into Scotland."

Her laughter was so fresh, honest. She took a drink of the whisky they had been sharing all evening and looked back at the obscene drawing. "So…ye know how to do some of these things, what ye've seen in this book." She said it like a statement instead of a question so he didn't answer, just smiled. "And," she looked at him, "ye've said ye'd like to teach me."

Will's eyebrows shot up. Had he said that?

"Teach me to throw the *sghian dubh*. So perhaps," her voice dropped, "ye could teach me a few other things as well. An independent woman should be knowledgeable."

Only a whore needed to know about the positions in Adela's book, and, bloody hell, there was no way he'd allow Jonet Montgomery to become a whore, but he wasn't going to argue with her if he would be her teacher. "My lessons could start right now," he said. "Though I don't have private quarters."

"I do," she said a bit breathlessly. "I can ask Ann to sleep with Margery and Jane and the bairns. I know she'd do it."

Will's heart thudded in him as parts of him woke instantly to the possibility of peeling the beautiful woman out of her clothes, showing her the wild ways of pure pleasure. He breathed deeply to gain control. "Jonet, 'tis the whisky talking." He shook his head. "I won't take you to bed when you aren't clearheaded."

She grabbed his shoulder and leveled him a stare. "Will Wyatt, I've been sipping whisky since I could walk. These are things I never knew existed, things I should know."

The woman put up a good argument, especially in his current physical state.

Jonet glanced around until she spied Ann talking to a couple Druim lads. "I'll meet ye in my room in quarter of an hour, and Will," she said and stood, a grin playing about her lips, "don't be late."

Chapter Seven

Jonet ran the rag, dampened with lilac-scented water, over her face, down her neck and chest. She rubbed her arms and dipped the cloth back in the basin. She grabbed the brush and worked it through her hair. It was clean as she'd bathed after waking from her nap before the bairn's blessing, but she wanted to brush the wood smoke from it. She barely noticed the snarls and stroked right through them.

What had she been thinking telling Will to meet her here, asking a giddy, shocked Ann to bunk somewhere else? *Hell.* It wasn't the whisky as she had an exceptional tolerance to any spirits. Perhaps it had been his drawings, the knowledge that there were other ways to lay with a man, other ways that had she known, may have kept Machar from straying.

The whoring lasses that had lured him easily away had called her cold, not able to keep her man. Well, now she would learn what it meant to keep one. She wasn't cold, just ignorant. She'd only been sixteen, and all her mother had told her was that her husband would teach her what she needed to know. Machar hadn't, but Will Wyatt was going to.

Jonet glanced at the brush full of her dark strands. If she kept it up, she'd be bald by the time he arrived. Lord, how many minutes had passed since she'd snuck through the nearly empty great hall to her room? Five minutes, ten? She raced to Ann's basin of fresh water and rubbed her teeth with a damp cloth and chewed some mint she kept from the kitchen garden. She sat on the edge of the bed and kicked off her boots. Should she be undressed? Nay, a man like Will might want to undress a lass. She stood up to bank the fire and paced along the rug. Maybe she should be lying on the covers. Nay, she didn't want to look like a whore. It was bad enough that she had invited him to her rooms. *God's teeth.* What to do? She'd already used the jake on the way up, and she'd washed, brushed, and drawn back the coverlet. There was nothing else to do but wait, so she stood in the center of the room doing nothing but trying not to faint.

A soft rap on the door made her jump, and before she could move, Will slid in and softly lowered the bar across it. Jonet forced herself to drop her clasped hands so they hung by her sides. Will walked directly to her and looked down into her eyes. If he asked her if she was sure she wanted to do this, she might back out.

"Kiss me." Her voice broke the nervous silence in the room.

Will's eyebrow rose, giving him the wicked look of a scoundrel, and Jonet's heart raced. "Aye now," he said low, his voice once again like velvet over pebbles. "I like a woman who tells me what she wants."

He lowered his face, his lips soft yet insistent, his hands

tangling through her hair to nudge her face to the side. With her first little moan, Will tasted her fully. She met his kiss with a building one of her own, plunging into the wild sensations his mouth provoked. Where else could that tongue work wonders? She shuddered on a pulse of lightning-fast heat.

His hands roamed with luxurious strokes and circles across her back and down her spine to cup her arse. She felt his upper arms bulge under her fingers as he lifted her to fit intimately against him. She gasped at the feel of him, so large, as he rubbed through her skirts, right where she ached. Lord, he probably knew all the places she ached.

"Oh Lord, Will," she rasped as his mouth kissed a hot path down her exposed neck. She tipped her head back to give him all the access he could want. "Ye're amazing."

He chuckled against her collarbone, then lowered her until her toes touched the floor. "And you're exquisite. We make a good pair." He inched her bodice down, and Jonet realized he'd unfastened all the ties and hooks down her back. Her gown slid off her body to pool in a whisper of wool and linen around her feet, leaving her in only a thin, white chemise. The heat from the flames warmed her back, and Will's solid body warmed her front. With each kiss and stroke, a fire heated her from within. Hot. She felt so hot.

His fingers stroked her bare shoulders, sliding under the lace edging there. He teased more kisses along her neck and back up to her lips, and Jonet only barely registered the *swoosh* of the undergarment joining her gown at her feet. Will leaned back for a moment, his eyes raking down her naked form. "God's teeth, Jonet," he groaned. "I've never seen such beauty before."

She held her breath as he stroked from her neck down

her skin to her breast. He palmed the weight, tweaking her peak, and she shut her eyes at the pure pleasure of his touch, of his praise. The more he caressed, the faster the fire ran through her, straight from his touch to deep within her pelvis until her legs felt weak. She must have leaned against him because he lifted her under the knees and, in two great strides, settled her down on the furs across the bed. He looked at her as she scooted up the bed to the top. The fur tickled across her skin, and she felt wild and naughty to be completely naked with him.

"Touch yourself," he said softly, and she raised her hand to her stomach to stroke a lazy circle up to capture her own breasts. She pinched one like he'd done, and he groaned, rubbing a hand down his torso to his own obvious arousal.

"It seems to me," she said, "that in all those sketches by the fire, the lass wasn't the only one naked."

In a flash of fabric, Will yanked his shirt off over his head, exposing his massive chest. Little scars crisscrossed his tan skin with one long line down the side of his tapered torso. He moved to the edge of the bed closest to her. She pointed to his pants. "How about those?"

He grinned at her boldness. "I didn't want to scare you."

She swallowed. "I'm no maid."

"Nay, you are not," he agreed and slowly untied his near-to-bursting trews. Before he was all the way undone, he crawled across the bed to kiss her. Jonet's eyes fluttered shut as the feelings once again heated through her. His kisses were so carnal, so hot and wet, and she loved them. He was uninhibited and demanded the same from her. And unlike with Machar, she responded—bloody hell, she responded! His strokes, his mouth, every part of Will attacked her worry, dissolving it into a stream of fire. There was no questioning or plotting on what to do next, only answering and moving to the natural impulses within her.

She heard his trews slide onto the floor and felt his naked body against her own. But instead of the nervous cold that had engulfed her at Machar's touch, Jonet dissolved into the warmth of sensation. He explored her nakedness. She laughed softly as he wiggled his finger into her naval, then shuddered as he moved lower.

Jonet stroked his broad shoulders and well-muscled arms. The power there would be intimidating with anyone else, but somehow, she trusted this wild man. She slid her palms down his back as he kissed her, marveling at the feel of his skin over strength, down to his bare arse. He growled in the back of his throat at her light exploration and moved his fingers, making her gasp as he touched places she didn't even know existed.

He left her mouth, trailing wet heat down her neck and chest to fasten his lips around her nipple. She gasped as he pulled and teased and felt her hips respond in a rhythm so natural she didn't need to think. She let her mind wander, taking in the achy pleasure tightening the muscles through her body. She tried to touch him. She should touch him, make him feel as good as he made her feel, but she kept losing her place as he stroked.

"Relax, Jonet," he whispered. "This is all about you."

"But it should be both ways," she said breathlessly.

"In time. Right now," he swallowed hard as if he were having trouble speaking for a moment, "let me show you the pleasure of loving."

He moved his strong fingers, and she groaned. "Let me

love you," he whispered and came up to kiss her panting lips. "You are so hot, Jonet."

She agreed completely. Heat coursed through her as her abdomen ached, coiling tighter and tighter toward some unknown conclusion. "Please," Jonet begged, though she didn't know what she pleaded for. "Will." She moaned and felt him shift over her, nudging her knees apart.

He kissed her again with wild heat, slanting and tasting and breathing into one another. He braced himself above her, his huge body engulfing her small form in the furs. Yet she didn't feel small. She felt large and alive and nearly bursting. He looked deeply into her eyes and drove into her. Jonet gasped, and he groaned. Full, so incredibly full.

"Good?" he asked.

"Aye, very good," she whispered, and he half smiled, half groaned again.

He started to move, and she wrapped her arms around him and met each thrust. Every sensation heightened the ache in her core. Kisses and strokes and Will's talented fingers worked across and within her body, tugging and luring, sliding and rocking, building the inferno higher.

"Will," she murmured against his lips as they raced together, two people moving as one. He reached down between their bodies and latched once again onto her nipple with his mouth. Her gasp rolled into a moan as Jonet felt the ache explode within her. Wave after wave of pleasure undulated along her body. In a heartbeat, Will followed her, his own deep voice filling the room as she continued her cry.

The pleasure continued to course through her as she held Will's body, her legs wrapped around his hips. After long moments, he carefully untangled her and rolled to his side, pulling her close into his chest as he kissed her head.

"Are you good?" he asked.

She took a few more breaths and felt him tense as if waiting for her answer. She glanced up into his eyes and smiled. "I don't think good describes how wonderful I feel."

He relaxed and kissed her damp brow. "I completely agree."

He watched her closely, and she propped up on one elbow. "And we didn't even do any of those things ye drew at the fire. That was," she glanced down their lengths, "the normal way of tupping."

He put his hands behind his head to lean back, looking up at her as her hair cascaded around them like a curtain. "That felt better than normal, don't you think?" he teased with a wink.

"Aye, but we didn't swing from ropes or any of that." Jonet couldn't understand how an act that had left her feeling so terrible with Machar had been so incredibly pleasurable with Will.

Will shook his head. "You don't need to do all those things to feel good, Jonet. You just need to let the fire consume you, let go and experience the feelings." That she had, because Will had led her there. She felt tears at the back of her eyes and blinked.

Will's smile fell, and he sat up, this thumb brushing under her eye. Hell, one of the tears must have broken free. "What's wrong?"

She shook her head. "I've just never felt so good before." She offered him a smile. "I had no idea it could be like that."

Will ran his fingers through her hair to cup her head. His smile returned. "Only with me, Jonet. Keep that in mind."

Was he teasing? His grin made it seem so. She smiled back. "So all those drawings, different positions, different places to put one's mouth, we won't be doing those things?"

He chuckled. "Nay, woman, we most certainly will be doing those things, too. I just thought we should start with the basics first." The words raced through her, bringing back a slight ache, but this time she knew what it was. Jonet reached up to wrap her hands around his neck, pulling him down for a kiss. She felt him stir against her and knew, without a worry, that they would get around to at least a few of those other things. It would be a long, wonderful night.

• • •

Will woke with the call of the cock somewhere down in the courtyard. He stretched his arms overhead and chuckled as he spied the light bruising of teeth Jonet had given his biceps hours ago during one of her peaks. He turned his head in the furs to see her dark hair spilling around her. She still slept, and he heard her soft breathing through parted lips. What a beauty. Soft and brave and full of life. And swiving with her was far beyond anything he'd ever experienced before. His Highland lass was lusty and strong, demanding and giving, oh was she giving… He'd been shocked by her desire to please him, wonderfully shocked. Would she blush when she woke? Would she pinken when he whispered to her through the day, reminding her of what they had shared, what they would share again? Because he planned to continue her lessons in pleasure. Him the master and her the student, though by morning, she was taking him to heights he'd never known before, had never known could exist.

He watched her slumber, her hair a mess of riotous curls, her dark lashes along her creamy skin. Aye, she should sleep. She must be exhausted after the hours of play. He should be tired, too, but watching her there filled him with energy as if he could climb the masts in seconds flat or swing across the deck on rope lines.

He chuckled then, seeing his rope tied to the bed frame overhead. She'd insisted they try one of the pictures he'd drawn, and he'd hurried to retrieve it, though they'd abandoned the position when she grew desperate.

The fur over her shoulder had slipped down, leaving the curve of her breast exposed. Another inch and her nipple would be a feast for his view. He tugged gently, and into the dull gray of dawn, the perfectly formed breast came. *Bloody hell.* How could he already be so hot for her again?

"See something ye like?" she whispered, bringing his gaze back to her eyes.

"Aye, very much," he said and gave her his infamously wicked grin. She pushed up on her elbow, letting the fur slide to her waist as she kissed him. Lord, she tasted like him mixed with her own sweet flavor. He inhaled in her hair, savoring the smell of their bodies together mixed with the faint smells of flowers and wood smoke.

She giggled. "How can ye be ready again?"

"I have no idea, not after satisfying my lusty woman all night."

She blushed then, and he winked so she'd know he teased. He shook his head, letting his grin turn to a real smile. "To tell you truth, Jonet, last night was the most lovely I've had."

"Really?" she asked, her eyes widening. "Ye're just

saying that."

"Nay, you are…remarkable."

Her smile grew slowly but surely until he knew she believed him. "Remarkable," she repeated. "And we didn't even get to do everything."

"Not yet," he finished. "I intend to be quite a task master." He kissed her then and snaked a palm over her hips to cup her luscious arse. She pushed back into his hand until he deftly found her. She gasped into his mouth and kissed him harder.

Bam! Bam! "Open up." A man pounded from the other side of the door.

"Bloody, swiving hell," Will cursed and stood up, grabbing his cutlass from the ground alongside the bed.

"It's Donald," Jonet said and sat up with the fur against her breasts.

"Jonet, I tried to stop him. He caught me sneaking in," Ann called through the door and Jonet cursed, making Will grin.

"Come back later," Jonet called.

"Is Will Wyatt in there with ye?" Donald asked.

Will looked at Jonet, and she nodded, her delicately arched brow raised over her laughing eyes. "Aye, Will Wyatt is definitely in here," Will called and chuckled at Donald's loud curse. The warrior was going to wake the keep.

"What goes on here?" another voice asked. Caden?

"Will has Jonet trapped in there," Donald called.

"Actually," Will called back, "I think it might be the other way around." Jonet's muffled laughter came from the hand she had slapped over her mouth.

"Open the door, Will," Caden commanded.

"You might want to give me a second to cover up, else Ann may get an unwelcome education," Will said and raised the bar.

He walked back to the bed to grab his trews from the floor but thought better of it. Instead, he crawled under the furs and hauled Jonet against his side, careful to completely cover her up to her chin. Her cheeks were red, but her eyes were sparkling like emeralds. He kissed her forehead and turned back to look at the door that crashed inward against the wall. Donald, Caden, and Ann barreled inside. Will's hand lay along the hilt of his cutlass, though he doubted there was really much threat.

Donald's eyes seemed to bulge from his red face. Ann held her hands to her cheeks though she smiled. Caden just shook his head, looking haggard. No doubt he wasn't getting much sleep with a new babe in his room.

"As ye can see," Jonet said from her fur shroud, "I'm perfectly fine."

"Well, I can't really see that," Donald said.

"And you won't," Will interjected.

Caden looked at Will's rope tied to the bed frame. He shook his head. "I won't even ask."

"'Tis probably a good thing," Will said with a huge grin.

Ann choked.

"What the devil were ye doing to her?" Donald insisted. The man definitely had a sweet inclination toward Jonet. Will's hand clasped the cutlass with ease.

"He was doing exactly what I wanted him to do," Jonet said and sat up straighter in the bed. "Which is none of yer concern, Donald."

Ann gasped, and Will looked to see where his love bites

had left feathery bruises along one of Jonet's shoulders. "He hurt ye," Donald said.

She glanced at her shoulder and shrugged. "No more than I hurt him."

Will couldn't keep his chuckles in and kissed the top of her head. "Aye, Jonet is a lusty woman. She needs a pirate to keep her in bliss."

"I'd say there's nothing cold at all about ye, Jonet," Ann said with a huge smile and nodded as if it was something she'd said before. Will wondered at the little message flying between the friends. Jonet was all fire and heat. How could she think herself cold?

"Well, I'm satisfied," Caden started.

"As am I," Will said and winked, making Ann snort.

Caden frowned. "Satisfied that no harm has been done here. Come, Donald, Ann, let's leave them alone." Caden glanced once more at the rope and shook his head as he heralded the other two out the door.

"I'll be back after I break my fast," Ann called through the door.

Jonet looked at him. "I wonder if Ruth and Lizzie will miss ye in the kitchens."

"Who?"

"The two giggly fools that strip ye naked with their gazes every time ye walk by them."

"Oh, that Ruth and Lizzie," he teased.

She leaned in with a kiss. "I don't want ye thinking about them at all," she murmured on his lips and slanted against him. The only thing Will could think about was the heat that once again shot through his blood.

. . .

Jonet braced her hands against the moss-covered boulder as she glanced over her shoulder at Will. Her skirts rolled up, a cool breeze whispered against her bare legs as he moved within her. He leaned over her back, nuzzling the hollow of her neck and shoulder.

"Ah, Jonet, I can't get enough of you."

"There's always more," she said.

He reached around her to palm her breasts that hung out of the top of her gown. She answered with a moan and strained to back into him, following the natural rhythm growing between them.

She panted as he increased the pace, his fingers moving down her torso to find the crux of her legs in front. The deep forest around them only allowed in splashes of sunshine. She focused on her fingers before her, digging into the rock. Would she crush it with her passionate strength?

Gripping and sliding, fiery dampness, Jonet hung her head as the world completely melted away into pure sensation. Will held her to him and loved her nape as he pumped harder, stroking with blissful pressure until she peaked.

"Will!" she called out, and he followed her with a deep growl at her ear. Her legs shook, but hc held them until the tremors slowly subsided. She laughed when he gallantly ran to the gurgling stream to fetch a wet rag to wash her.

She turned to him, her face flushed and full of joy. "I think that's one of my favorite so far." She slowly loaded her breasts back into the tight confines of her gown and laughed at the look of longing that furrowed Will's face. "They need some time out of the wind."

He caught her to him and kissed her gently as the breeze tugged at the curls around her face. Jonet's heart soared. He cared for her. He must. The way he touched her made her feel as if her happiness was all that mattered.

Will grabbed her hand and the sack they'd packed with food for their private meal by the stream. They walked back toward Munro Castle, fingers intertwined.

"Jonet?"

"Mmmm?"

"Have you thought about children?" he asked, and she nearly stumbled.

"I think about children all the time," she said. "I'm surrounded by them and love them dearly." She laughed softly. What did he mean?

"With all our loving over this fortnight," he squeezed her hand, "are you worried at all that you'll conceive?"

Lord, how long had she prayed for a child? The entire time Machar had been alive and then in her dreams. "I…I don't know if I can," she answered truthfully. "I didn't conceive when I was married."

Meg had told Jonet that she thought she felt healthy, but Jonet hadn't asked her specifics about her bairn-making capabilities. There had been no need since she was already a widow when Meg came to Druim.

"You were so young then," Will said. "But if you…had my babe within you—"

"I would be completely happy," she answered truthfully.

Will smiled broadly at her and nodded. He opened his mouth as if to continue, but then looked forward again, remaining silent. They walked for several quiet minutes. Jonet inhaled the sweet, spring air and listened to the birds overhead. Life was lovely and so full of potential. Perhaps she could conceive Will's child. The thought fluttered in her stomach. She'd love it with all her heart. Would it be enough, though, when he left for the sea? The thought doused some of her joy, and she pushed it aside.

"Stephen has seemed troubled," Will said as the village came into view.

"More than usual?" Jonet asked of the frown-wearing lad that had come with Will from the sea. The lad doted on Charissa but didn't try to make friends with any others.

Will nodded. "I think he's had trouble with some of the Munro boys. They tease him for not knowing how to ride."

"Neither did ye," she pointed out.

"Aye, but I have other talents." He winked at her but grew serious again. "He wants desperately to return to the *Queen Siren*."

"Ye will go soon then?" she asked, trying to keep the sadness from her voice.

Will shrugged. "As far as I know, there is still a huge bounty on my head, but Stephen could possibly return if I found a way to get him to Captain Bart."

Jonet nodded, a little bit relieved. Her happiness wouldn't end this day. "I want to check on the girls. Margery and Jane have been working so well together. The little ones barely need me."

He kissed her head. "Oh, they need you." It was such a sweet gesture that she felt tears burn at the back of her eyes. Or was that from the nagging thought that he wouldn't be there forever? Lord, help her. She was falling in love.

. . .

Will left her with a quick kiss and a whispered promise that he'd think on their next adventure. The woman was insatiable. She seemed determined to try every erotic position and wheedle out every pleasurable possibility either of them could think of. He grinned and shook his head. She nearly tired him out. But that wasn't what kept those emerald eyes and lush smile forefront in his mind. It was everything that made up Jonet Montgomery. The way she cared and loved those children and jumped in to help her people. Aye, his Highland lass had a full heart and a full dose of energy. And bravery…he chuckled. Brave enough to try anything he whispered and trusting enough to surrender herself to his every caress. Will inhaled the cool, fresh air free of the taint he usually ignored in port. The mountains in the distance presented a fabulous backdrop to this secluded world. God's teeth, he could hide out here forever. He frowned suddenly over the thought.

"There ye are," Searc called from the bailey.

"Have you seen Stephen?" Will asked as he came up to him and Caden. Caden held his newborn son over one shoulder and gently patted his back. The Macbain leader's hair was sticking up in patches, and there was a milky stain of spit up down one of his sleeves. "You look like a new papa, Caden," Will said and laughed. Searc grinned.

Caden frowned at them but kissed his son's tiny head as he cupped it and changed shoulders. "Meg is catching up on her sleep for a few hours. Kincaid is quite active at night."

"Sounds like the lad has promise," Will teased, and Searc

choked.

"Speaking of promise with the ladies," Caden said. "Where is Jonet?" Searc sobered, and they both stared at Will. Was he in trouble?

He nodded back toward the village. "She went to check on the children with Margery and Jane. Have you seen Stephen? I wanted to talk with him."

"Haven't seen him since early this morning," Searc said. "So are ye planning to wed Jonet?"

Will looked between the two Highlanders. "Well now, I don't believe that is your concern."

"Actually," Caden said. "It is. I am her chief, and she is without husband or family to care for her. Therefore, she falls under my concern." Searc nodded, his lips tight.

"Is marriage a consequence of swiving with a woman here?"

Caden stared at him. If he didn't have a babe attached lovingly to his shoulder, he'd look downright murderous. "Jonet could get her heart broken when ye leave. Lasses get attached. She's not a whore ye can just leave in port."

Fury poured through Will. "Of course she isn't. She's nothing like a whore."

"I'm glad we're all agreed," Searc said. "We just want ye to remember that."

Will ran his hand through his hair. Of course he knew that. The thought of leaving Jonet sickened his stomach, but what could he do? Stop touching her? Impossible. Wed her and take her to the *Queen Siren*? Impossible. Captain Bart would never allow a woman not raised at sea to live on ship, and neither would Will. It was dangerous and difficult, even for salty seamen, let alone a flower like his Highland lass.

But he couldn't remain here in this foreign land. His life was at sea. There was no way around it. Eventually, he'd have to surrender Jonet.

"I promised Cook I'd come up with something for supper," Will grumbled and walked past them. Maybe Stephen was hiding out in the kitchens with Ruth and Lizzie. The girls had begun to flirt with the boy a bit. He frowned over that, too. He'd have to warn the young lad away from that pair of trouble. They seemed every bit as diabolical as some of Adela's girls.

Will spent the rest of the afternoon helping Cook come up with an interesting way to season venison and cook some wild onions to complement it. The large woman was full of good humor and kept him working hard, yet his mind kept straying to Jonet. And even though Caden and Searc had deftly pointed out a tangled problem, just the thought of her sweet face was a balm to the aching head the two Highlanders had given him. As he lifted the pot of boiled onions from the hearth, Ruth came up to him.

"Will," she whispered near his ear. "Eric says he wants to talk with ye about Jonet."

"Oh?"

She nodded and glanced around. "He wants ye to meet him in the back cellar after the meal to talk. Just men. No swords."

What was the clodpoll up to? "Very well," Will answered, and Ruth smiled.

Will didn't mention the meeting to Jonet as they ate together in the great hall with Meg and Ann, Caden, Searc, and the rest. Everyone seemed to like the seasoning on the meat and onions. Will wondered how the crew was getting on with Pete's routine fare. Maybe they would appreciate his creative cooking after eating the same fish stew for months.

Eric didn't come to supper, and Ruth left with Lizzie early on. Perhaps the giggly young women had finally stopped trying to entice him into their bed.

"I need to…talk with Stephen," Will told Jonet. "I still haven't caught up with the lad. I wonder if he's sulking somewhere."

"I'll help the girls get the little ones ready for bed," Jonet said.

He nodded and winked. "I'll think of something for us to do later."

Her smile reached her gorgeous eyes, and the heat from her gaze warmed his middle. "Later then," she said and turned to head out with Ann. Caden and Meg rose with little Kincaid, and Searc walked out with the other warriors to finish their duties for the night.

The three elderly council members sat at the table, observing everything. Angus took a long drink of ale. He seemed a little unsteady. Perhaps that batch of brew was strong. "Jonet is a lovely lass," Angus said, and Bruce agreed heartily.

"Loves those children as her own," Bruce said. "Too bad she has none of her own blood, not that it's her fault." He elbowed Old Kenneth, whose one good eye seemed to again take Will's measure.

"She was married for a year?" Will asked casually. No one seemed to like to talk about Jonet's past, including her.

"A little more," Kenneth said. "Almost two, if I think on it."

"And no children? Perhaps her husband wasn't very

interested," Will said, throwing out the bait.

Angus snorted. "That man was interested in anything draped with a skirt."

Will didn't move, just raised an eyebrow. "He stepped out on her?"

"The man tupped every female that would have him, and there were many," Angus supplied and hiccupped. "And didn't father even one bastard. Me thinks that his seed was dead."

"Poor Jonet," Bruce added and shook his head. "Stuck with a scoundrel and didn't even get a bairn from it."

Will sat back, taking in this new information. Jonet must have known her husband was unfaithful. That would explain her easy jealousy over flirting lasses.

Kenneth took a sip of his own ale. "Someone courting her needs to know she'll have nothing to do with a man who plants himself in other fields." He narrowed his eyes.

Warning received. Did Jonet know she had so many papas looking out for her? Will nodded and stood. He really needed to talk with her about her past. It could very well be affecting how she felt about him. But first he had a meeting with Eric.

• • •

Jonet left the cottage where the bairns were nearly asleep. Margery and Jane had become best of friends it seemed. She smiled. What would she do without Ann? Aye, it was good to have a confidante. She walked into the empty great hall. Where was Ann? She climbed the stone steps to their room and stopped when she saw a scrap of parchment skewered to the door with a small dagger.

She smiled wickedly and yanked the blade to free the note. The letters scrawled across the small leaf were uneven, hastily written.

> *Come to the last empty stable stall for our next adventure. Will*

Jonet hastened into the room to wash and freshen her teeth. Adventure? The word sent a thrill through her to the pit of her stomach. The man and his adventures were amazing. He'd opened a whole world of passion for her, and she loved it. Hopefully, he was enjoying their romps as well. He seemed to be. The happy flipping in her stomach tightened into an ache. What if he grew bored of her? Bloody hell, she wouldn't let that happen again. Not this time, not when she was falling in love.

Jonet brushed her hair and chewed one last piece of mint before sliding on silent feet out of her door. She didn't want to keep Will waiting. Her heart sped up as she walked across the dark bailey, her slippers crunching on the pebbles. The smell of fresh straw made her smile at the memory of the kiss he'd given her there. That was before they'd… She heard a sound way back in the dark stable.

"Och, Will, that feels so good," came a breathless moan. Jonet froze, her whole body contracting into one solid ache. She took a few steps closer until she heard the jolting sound of skin slapping against skin.

"Lizzie, leave some of him for me." Ruth giggled.

Could she be really hearing this? Was this the adventure he had planned? Was she not enough to keep him from straying?

"Will, oh Will," Lizzie crooned and let out the breathless moans of one reaching her peak. His own growls of pleasure tore through Jonet's heart. No words, just deep, guttural moans of pleasure.

"Now me," Ruth insisted. "I'll show ye what that cold fish, Jonet, never can."

The terrible words slapped across Jonet. Her hands flew up to her hot cheeks. Tears streamed down as she backed up. Whispers from the time of Machar rose up in her head. They'd haunted her for seven years, but now they reared up to pierce her soul. No matter what she did, she was undesirable. Even when she thought, when she'd hoped… Jonet turned and stumbled right into a broad chest.

Chapter Eight

What the bloody devil was going on? Will caught Jonet to him in the darkness. She was sobbing uncontrollably. He could hear his name being exalted from back in the stables.

That son of a whore, Eric, had locked him in the farthest back larder behind the kitchens. He'd still be stuck there if he hadn't learned to carry a small pick on himself since his time locked in the Tower of London. He'd worried over Eric's foul plan and ran to find Jonet. It wasn't until he found the slip of parchment in her room, a note that he hadn't written, that he knew to look in the stables.

"Jonet," he said and leveled her frantic eyes on his. "I'm here. I'm not in there." He could clearly hear the sounds of two women calling his name as some bastard pleasured them. Eric, no doubt, and the two fool girls from the kitchen. He must have told them to call Will's name. His face heated as he realized just how guilty he would have looked if he hadn't found her while they were in the act.

She still stood rigid as if in shock. "Jonet, 'tis Eric trying to turn you against me. I'm right here. He locked me in the larder, but I'm here."

She nodded, her inhale full of trembles. "I…I just need to be alone."

She pulled back. He didn't want her to go, not so upset, but he released his hold on her and followed her out of the stables. Donald, Gavin, and Searc stood talking in the bailey as Jonet ran past them like the devil was chasing her.

"What the bloody hell?" Donald called and leveled a piercing gaze on Will.

"Don't fucking look at me," Will threw at them and pointed back toward the stables. "It's that whoreson, Eric, and those two Munro lasses in there pretending I'm sleeping around on Jonet. If I hadn't escaped the bloody kitchen where Eric locked me up, Jonet would believe it, too."

The men walked to the stable doors. Will heard Donald curse.

"I'd ship those two lasses off to a whore house before they meddle with the wrong bloke," he called and turned to go after Jonet. She'd run into the castle, probably to her room. He charged up the stairs. She'd asked to be alone, but the more he thought about it, the more he couldn't let the night end like that. He slammed on the door with his fist and tried the latch. The door wasn't barred, and he pushed into the room and stopped.

Jonet sat before the low embers of an old fire in a puddle of her skirts, her head bent. Her shoulders shook. Will shut the door behind him and barred it. He didn't want anyone interrupting them. He walked over and knelt beside her, but she didn't look up.

He stirred the fire until it came back to life and added some peat from the box next to the hearth. It flared up, and slices of light flickered against Jonet's brilliant, black hair.

"Jonet," he said softly.

She shook her head. "I can't do it," she whispered.

"Do what?"

"I'm just a cold fish."

"What the bloody hell are you talking about? Did someone call you that?"

She nodded. "Everyone, back when Machar was alive," she said numbly. "He —"

"Was an idiotic fool who I wish was alive so I could slice him in two," Will said. "You are no cold fish, Jonet Montgomery. You are warm with a golden heart." He crawled to sit in front of her. "You are hot and lush and full of adventure, in and out of bed. Anyone who calls you cold is plainly lying."

She shook her head. "I didn't know anything about entertaining a man when he was alive."

"You were young, a virgin when you wed him."

Jonet nodded.

"You weren't supposed to know anything about entertaining a man," he continued. Will's fists ached at his sides. What he wouldn't give to have that damn bastard in front of him. "A proper husband would have schooled you privately, slowly, showing you all the pleasures of love."

"One time," she looked back down, "he said he'd teach me." She swallowed hard. "He took me to watch him with two other girls."

Goddamned bastard of a swiving jackal! Will held his tongue and forced himself to breathe. "What happened,

Jonet?" he said slowly, softly.

"He wanted me to join them." Fresh tears dripped down onto her hands in her lap. "I wouldn't. He laughed at me. One of the girls called me a cold fish. The name stuck."

"I'll kill anyone that calls you that," Will swore with such vehemence that Jonet glanced up. "It's a lie, and it hurts you. I won't stand to let anyone hurt you again."

Fresh tears broke out of her, and she choked on an inhale. Enough with leaving her alone. Will pulled her into his arms, cradling her against his chest as she sobbed. He rocked gently like he'd done with frightened children on the ship, keeping his fury at their mistreatment in check. Bloody devil, one didn't have to be stuck in a slave-trading ship to be abused.

"Is that why…?" he said and paused. "Why you've been so…adventurous in loving me?"

"I didn't want to lose ye," she said, crying harder. He tucked her head under his chin and kissed the soft hair there.

After a long moment, she calmed down a bit.

"You certainly seemed to enjoy swiving with me," he whispered. Could she have been pretending with him?

She looked up. "I did, I do, every second." Her eyes looked even greener with the fire lighting their watery depths. "'Tis truth, I've never felt so wonderful before."

He smiled. "Well then, you're not a cold fish. Perhaps a tired one, perhaps a bit tender now," he said. "But definitely not cold."

He ran his thumb over the lines furrowing her forehead, smoothing the worry away. "Jonet, you are the most beautiful, passionate woman I've ever met in all my wanderings on this earth. I am honored to know you and flaming hot to bed you, and only you."

She studied him and sniffed.

"I pledge it on my honor," he said. More words sat on his tongue, words he swore he'd never utter because they were for fools. But they were there.

She smiled, and he breathed. He didn't have to say them.

She nestled back into his chest. "Yer the most amazing man I've ever encountered. And I'm flaming hot for ye, too."

He chuckled and held her close, his heart full. He pushed aside all thoughts of the future, all regrets of the past and focused on the warm, sweet woman in his arms. "My sweet Jonet," he whispered, and as she glanced up, he met her lips, telling her with his kiss the words he wouldn't say.

• • •

Jonet and Will walked hand in hand through the bailey toward the houses where their children were sleeping. Ann had stayed with them again, giving the couple an ample opportunity for a private night together. Even though there had been passion, Will had refused to let her do anything to pleasure him.

Tonight is all about you, Jonet, he'd whispered in the firelight, his hot kisses and caresses running down her feverish body. She blushed in the sunlight as she remembered the intimate details.

"I love your pink cheeks," he whispered by her ear. "I hope it means you're thinking about swiving with me."

"Always," she said with a confident smile. As they passed the stables, her grin faltered. "What happened after I left?"

He shrugged. "Searc, Caden, and Donald handled it.

Those two sluts would make fabulous whores. I should send them back with Captain Bart to introduce to Adela." He'd never wanted to throttle women before, but they best not get in his way any time soon. "And if Donald or Caden didn't do something about Eric, the man won't live the day."

She squeezed his arm. "Let's just check to see how the children are this morning before ye go off plotting murder."

"Bloody too late. I've already planned a hundred ways to kill the bastard." He kissed her quickly while they walked. "And after that, I plan to boast to every Macbain and Munro how hot you are in my bed."

She gasped and slapped his arm. "Ye wouldn't."

"Not a soul will ever utter your name and the word cold in the same breath again."

"But what if it's snowing, and I forgot my cloak?" she teased.

"Then I'll just have to kiss you until you burn enough to change the snow to rain."

"So poetic," she said.

"I can make it into a rhyme." He lifted his eyebrows up and down until she laughed heartily.

"Will!" Charissa yelled and launched herself at his legs as they walked into the crowded cottage. He caught her up in a hug and kissed her cheeks soundly. He placed her on his shoulders where she nearly strangled him with her little legs.

"Where is Stephen?"

Margery and Jane exchanged looks. "He didn't come back here last night," Margery said.

"What happened?" Jonet asked and hugged a small boy.

"He was really angry about not being able to climb onto a horse. Some of the boys teased him," Margery said. "And I made a mess of things." She looked down at her hands and nodded.

"What did you do?" Will asked.

"I hit him," Margery said.

"Ye hit Stephen for not mounting a horse?" Jonet asked.

"Nay, the other boy."

"She punched that bully Peter right in his nose," Jane said.

Will noticed the dark bruises on Margery's knuckles. He took Charissa from his shoulders and knelt before the brave girl. She'd been raised in London streets and knew a thing or two about brawling. Dory, unfortunately, wasn't here to heal her this time. "Well, I'd say you probably gave him a thing or two to consider," Will said and ran his thumb gently over the fingers. None seemed broken. "We should get you up to see Meg."

"Stephen was so furious," Margery said. "Like I'd somehow made him seem weak for sticking up for him." Her face began to get blotchy. "Stupid boy," she said, but guilt lay heavy in her eyes.

"And he hasn't come home since," Jane finished.

Home? This wasn't Stephen's home. The boy had made it perfectly clear that he didn't consider any part of Scotland his home.

"I need to find him," he said to Jonet.

"We will find him."

She must have seen the argument brewing in his face because she raised a hand toward him. "We'll get farther faster on my horse."

"Your horse? I believe Bart is my horse," he said. He loved to watch the spark of unguarded irritation in her eyes.

It meant that she trust him not to leave her over some little argument. He smiled over the victory.

"Just because ye named it doesn't make it yers. Ye can't even ride it well."

He laughed. "Watch it, or Margery will punch ye in the nose."

The girl turned brighter red but smiled when he winked at her.

"He might still be in the village or castle," Jonet said and handed the little boy back to Jane. "Let's start up at the castle."

They jogged next to each other back toward the bailey. Noise ahead drew Will's attention.

"Now where's that ale-swilling brother of mine?"

Dory? Jonet and he ran under the spiked portcullis and stopped before the small group of dismounting Scots and his sister.

"Ewan?" Jonet said. "Is the plague over?"

Will noticed the older man and woman from the mad dash to Munro Castle, Searc's parents. Searc was helping his mother down from her steed.

"There are a few who are still recovering," Lady Munro said. "But thanks to God for our gifts," she smiled at Dory, "even the worst are soon to be walking again."

Dory looked thinner and tired, but she smiled beautifully at the woman. Ewan held her gently in front of him.

"When a visitor came looking for ye," Ewan said, his gaze on Will, "Alec and I thought it a good time for our wives to take a deserved break."

From behind another old warrior that had returned with them, stepped a medium-sized, scraggly-bearded fellow.

"Seems me Panda is fitting right in here," Captain Bart said.

"Captain," Will said, a huge smile lifting his worry for a moment. He caught the old man in a hug.

"Now, lad, put these bones down. I've been jostled enough on that wagon seat."

"Is everything well with the *Queen Siren*?" Will asked, his gaze flitting to Dory, but she just smiled.

"Aye, but purely boring without you there. The crew bemoans Pete's stew, and no one can keep a rhythm like you—"

"Says all the ladies," Dory and Bart finished his usual phrase at the same time. Will just shook his head. Hopefully, Jonet would find the saying as foolishly fun as it was meant to be. Her little grin allowed his own.

"So, lad," Captain Bart continued, "you been having a grand time with the Highland lasses?" His eyes strayed to Jonet, an eyebrow raised. Leave it to Bart to poke the most sensitive spot in the room.

"Actually, just one Highland lass. Jonet Montgomery, meet Captain Bartholomew Wyatt, my father."

She dipped a little curtsy. "Pleased to meet ye."

"Well now, Panda, did you see that curtsy? Just as graceful as a London lady." He nodded to Jonet.

"I'm graceful," Dory said, a streak of stubbornness in her tone.

"Aye, she is," Ewan confirmed and hugged her closer. Somehow, the overt display of affection didn't irritate Will anymore. In fact, he rather liked the show of love Ewan displayed for Dory. He was an honorable man. Ewan's eyes narrowed with suspicion as Will smiled at him. *Bloody hell.* Hadn't he ever smiled at the man?

"Will," Jonet said softly. "Stephen."

"Blast," Will cursed. "Captain, we'll have to visit when I return. The boy from O'Neil's ship seems to be missing."

"When was he last seen?" Searc asked.

"Last night, but he didn't sleep in the cottage he was assigned," Jonet said. "We were about to start a search in the castle."

"Aye, find the boy," Bart said. "This concerns him, too."

"What concerns him?" Will asked.

Captain Bart smiled broadly. "I've come to take you home to the *Queen Siren*."

• • •

Jonet wrapped her arms around Will's middle as they rode through the damp forest. A quick check of the castle and village hadn't uncovered Stephen, so the small search party had split up to comb the surrounding forests and mountain passes. Even though they rode in silence broken occasionally by calling the lad's name, Jonet's mind whirled. *Home to the* Queen Siren. There hadn't been time to question the pirate captain, but the man had seemed confident that Will could leave Scotland. Leave Scotland and leave her.

Jonet's stomach turned in on itself, and it was all she could do to hold back the sob that threatened to explode from her. *Bloody hell!* She'd just found him, found the freedom to enjoy a man, an honorable, caring man. She blinked to quell the tears.

"I can't imagine what has changed that would make it safe for me to return to sea," Will said. Jonet's eyes widened. Could he read her mind? He ran a hand across hers and glanced over his shoulder. "Your heart is pounding into my back, and you haven't said a word." He grinned at her, and she let her eyes close and smashed her face into his back.

"The crew must miss ye. And yer father," she mumbled, her fingers curling into his shirt. "And ye must miss the sea."

"I know the sea," he said and shook his head. "All this earth and green."

"Ye're already riding a horse," she pointed out. "Charissa seems to really enjoy running through the wildflowers. And everyone loves yer cooking."

And someone here loves you, she wanted to scream. Aye, love. She swallowed hard but couldn't keep the single tear from running down her cheek. The thought of Will leaving back to the sea without her…it tore at her, physically hurt.

"Aye," he said. "True. Like I said, though, the captain might be a bit too hasty. I have to hear why he thinks it's safe. King Henry still has a bounty set on my head, as far as I know. I assumed I'd hide for a year or more. After all, I made a pledge to help put a new roof on your orphan's home."

"Aye, ye did."

Will looked through the dense forest. "Stephen! Come out, lad!"

Jonet forced herself to breathe. Nothing was determined yet. She still had him here, and a year was a long time. She hugged him tightly, and he ran a hand over her arm.

"Stephen!" His deep voice barreled through the undergrowth. "Where are you, lad?"

Jonet watched the ground as they passed, searching for signs. Broken twigs, a print in the mud, anything to tell them they were headed in the right direction. "Why do ye think he ran away?" she asked.

"Margery embarrassed him, but it was more than that." Will glanced left, then right. "The boy feels he doesn't belong here. He was raised at sea and taken against his will. He's angry." He breathed fully, Jonet feeling the widening of his chest. "Captain Bart would be good for him."

"Were ye an angry boy?"

Will chuckled darkly. "Obnoxiously so, but the captain wouldn't put up with it. Got me playing drums and threw me down in the kitchens when I couldn't keep my opinions to myself."

"So ye learned to cook." She smiled against his back. How like her pirate not to just wallow in anger but to do something productive.

"Aye. At first I threw everything that wasn't poison together in hopes of making them regret putting me down there. The first couple of meals were horrible."

She laughed. "When did ye start trying to make something good to eat?"

"After they made me eat my own concoction."

She chuckled against his back. "Why didn't ye run away?"

"I was stuck on ship. Nowhere to run away to at sea." He held a hand cupped to his mouth. "Stephen! Answer me, lad! Captain Bart's here; we can go home!"

Her stomach ached like he'd hit her in the gut. From laughter to paralyzing worry with one phrase. Lord, she needed to toughen herself.

They rode for a few more silent minutes. "Before the captain came along," Will said slowly, "I didn't have a home."

"He found ye like the children ye save, right?"

Will nodded. "In the stinking hull of a slave ship,

shackled and forgotten. I was too dangerous to keep up on deck. I caused havoc. Even the other children didn't talk to me for fear of being beaten for knowing me. I was alone. I know what alone feels like."

Lord, so did she. So alone for so many years. She'd finally found Ann and some friends. Aye, she knew. "Stephen!" she yelled. "Stephen!"

Will angled the horse up a thin path. "This seems to be traveled more." He pointed to a broken twig on a bush.

"It's fresh, see the green," Jonet said. "Someone's passed here over the last day."

Will looked up where the path wound. "Into the mountains?"

"There are caves up there," Jonet said. "Caves with huge drops in the dark, pits that could kill a man. Stephen!"

"Blast," Will cursed. "That's bloody hell where I'd go." He urged the horse forward faster, and Jonet noticed more broken twigs and a few footprints in the soft soil. A ray of sun caught Jonet's eye. It was going down. Soon the path would be cast in shadows.

"These mountains are not safe at night," Jonet said and yelled again for the boy.

"And he may have been out here last night," Will said. "Damn it all, I should have watched him closer."

Jonet rubbed his back, her face heating with guilt. If he hadn't been so concerned about her, he may have paid closer attention to Stephen. "I'm sorry," she whispered.

He turned in his seat to look down at her, his thumb coming up to her cheek. Lord, was there a tear there? He wiped across it, frowning. "You're crying."

"I didn't mean to keep ye away from the children."

"Hmmm…would I rather spend time wooing a lovely Highland lass or convincing a foul-tempered lad to give this life a chance?" He shook his head. "Jonet, you have nothing to be sorry for. The boy is old enough not to wander off. He made his own stupid choice. We are just going to try to save him from it."

"Like Captain Bart saved ye," she said.

He cupped the side of her cheek and brushed a kiss across her lips. "Aye, like the captain saved my sorry arse."

They rode farther up into the mountain terrain calling for Stephen, and the sun rays continued to lengthen until they disappeared behind the range. A movement to the right in the underbrush caught Jonet's eye. Will stiffened and pulled the horse to a halt. They sat still in the shadows. Jonet felt Will unsheathe his dagger.

A pair of yellow eyes stared at them from the woods, and the hairs on her nape stood up. Wolf. "Is it Meg's pet?" Will asked.

"I don't know," she whispered. "It travels alone or with its mate," she said glancing around at the darkness.

Will clicked to the horse, and it moved forward. The wolf followed alongside without attacking or running off. It made a whining noise, and Will stopped Bart again. The horse's ears flicked nervously, and he sidestepped. Will held the reins tight.

"All right, you have our attention," Will said evenly and looked directly at the beast. The wolf came out from the shadows into the twilight. It was huge and gray with seemingly soulless eyes.

Jonet gasped softly. "That's Meg's wolf. She calls him Nickum."

"A Gaelic name?"

"Aye, it means mischievous."

Will chuckled softly. "Well, then we should get along fine. What do you want, Nickum?"

The wolf whined and trotted off to the left a ways, stopped, and looked back at them.

"I think he wants ye to follow him," Jonet said.

"Seems like it," Will said, shaking his head. "Do you know where Stephen is? God's teeth, I'm talking to a blasted wolf." After clicking and cajoling, the horse, Bart, finally moved off the main path to follow the wolf into the darkening forest. The sound of a waterfall could be heard up ahead. Would a thirsty boy have heard it?

Nickum made sure they were following and led them at a fast pace around bushes and trees until the sound of falling water made it difficult to hear anything else. The trees opened up, and the shadows lessened so that they could make out a ledge and a series of rocks and waterfalls down into a dark basin below.

"Stephen!" Will's voice cut through the roaring power of the thawing springwater running off the mountain.

Nickum ran ahead, his nimble feet carrying him to a cliff that leaned out over the falls. Moist, chilled air hovered around them as they dismounted. Will grabbed his rope off the saddle. Jonet tied Bart to a tree and followed Will up the slick, moss-covered rocks and dirt. He continued to call for the boy. Nickum barked low in his throat, his nose pointed to a rock outcropping below a pool of water that must have been created by eons of mountain water carving away at the rock. A lump lay on the outcropping, water coursing around it.

Jonet could scarcely say it, but she didn't have to.

"Bloody hell, Stephen!" Will yelled and leaped up into the carved pool of frigid water. The boy must have fallen from it onto the outcropping. If he'd continued down the slope… Jonet shivered as she looked straight below into the dark abyss of plunging water.

"Be careful!" Jonet yelled, but her words were swallowed in the constant, rushing roar.

Will waded to the edge of the rock pool above the boy. The drop was too far to reach. He looked all around, turning in a tight circle and stopped as he studied a wide-spreading tree overhead.

"Nay," Jonet said softly.

But Will quickly knotted the end of his rope and threw it up toward a thick branch. The rope splashed back in the water, and he fished it out, trying two more times before getting the rope all the way over the limb. He jumped up and grabbed the dangling end and tugged. The rope caught on the branch overhead, and he tied the end together with an intricate knot that slid when pulled.

"Will!" she yelled, her hands clasped. He looked to her and nodded, their gazes connecting in the last light of day. He knew to be careful. She held her breath as he tied the rope around his waist and began to lower down to the boy. He controlled the descent with the other end. She'd never seen anything like it. Jonet watched where she stood along the bank, her slippers wet in the moss and mud. A little farther. She held her breath as Will reached the stone outcropping. As soon as he stepped down, he grabbed the boy, lifting him like a sack of wet grain over his shoulder.

Jonet couldn't tell if the boy was breathing. He certainly

didn't look to be conscious. How long had he been out there in the freezing water? Nickum stood near the rope in the above pool. They would have ridden right past the waterfall if the wolf hadn't stopped them.

Jonet leaned forward, watching Will struggle to climb up the rope with Stephen over his shoulder. He slipped, the tie around his waist catching him. Jonet shuddered and ran up to stand with Nickum. Could she reach the boy if Will lifted him to her?

"Will," she yelled down and waded into the water. The current yanked at her heavy wool skirts, sending chills all over her body. It was freezing, but she was already wet, and she wasn't going to let Will struggle alone. She grabbed the taut rope and made her way to the edge, her feet catching and sliding on the rocks below the surface. How the hell had he walked out there so effortlessly?

Will yelled at her, but she couldn't hear. She closed in and leaned down to offer her hands. She panted in the icy water, her legs already numbing. Stephen's head brushed her fingertips, and she started grabbing at air until she felt something to hold onto. The boy's shirt collar. Jonet reversed her pull, tugging the boy with all her power. She pushed underwater with her feet against the rocks, backing up. Nickum came closer and bit into the boy's collar, his massive strength much more than Jonet's.

Jonet let go as Nickum continued to pull his limp body to the edge. She felt the boy's warmth as he passed. Thank the Lord, he was alive.

She stood up, trying to see Will as he pulled on the rope, the branch overhead bending. Could he get up? Should she help him? She waded back over, his yells lost in the water.

"Will, can I help?" she called, and her foot caught in a crevice. She fell forward, splashing into the water. The icy flow engulfed her, and she gasped, inhaling water. The pain in her chest burned with ice, and she flailed, jerking her legs, trying to get her feet under her again to push upward. As her foot came dislodged, the current that had been building behind her took over, slamming her forward.

Jonet screamed, a gurgling cry as the mountain water carried her, bumping and scraping over the ledge, over and down into the black abyss.

• • •

The scream echoed through Will's head. *Jonet!* Her body fell over the ledge he'd just handed Stephen up to. He leaped toward her. His fingers brushed numbly along her form as she continued in the sweep of water. "Nay!" he roared, louder than the rush around him. "Nay! Jonet!" But she was gone into the dark waterfall below.

Could she even swim? Was she even conscious to try to fight the deep eddies he'd seen as they ran along the edge to reach Stephen? Time seemed to be rushing by as fast as the black water while his mind worked too slow. He had to reach her, had to save her. Nothing else mattered.

With a quick glance to see Stephen on the dry edge with Nickum, Will lowered down as far as the doubled line of rope would go. It bit into his middle. He unsheathed his dagger from his calf and straightened as much as he could. With one slice, the rope snapped. He threw the dagger from himself just as he plummeted, his arms around his head.

Water engulfed him as he hit, and he sunk until he could

straighten and kick toward the surface. Blinded by the dark, he thrashed his arms around, searching for a warm body. He surfaced and gasped a lungful of air while kicking off his boots. He glanced around frantically, desperate to see. What if he couldn't find her? What if she never smiled or laughed at him again. What if the spark in her eyes were dulled, frozen in d— Nay. He wouldn't think it. His chest burned, his body numb in the cold. Still he pushed his arms against the currents, waving them underwater. *God, help me find her!* Had he ever prayed before? Not since those days long ago in the slaver's hold. *God, please!*

There! Something floated in the foam. He kicked off, powerful strokes cutting through the black water toward the object. His fingers sank into wet wool, and he turned Jonet until her face was above water. Her pale face looked lifeless, her black hair a tangling of floating silk. Keeping her face above the surface, Will kicked to the bank, his toes catching in the rocky incline. He carried her out of the icy flow and onto the forest floor, dropping in exhaustion and panic.

"Jonet," he called, brushing strands from her face. Her lids were closed, dark lashes wet spikes against her skin. "Oh God, please Jonet." He ran his hands over her body, willing it to move. He lay his palm on her chest where a fast beat unhitched the lump in his throat. He turned her on her side and slapped against her back several times.

Pete had pushed air into a lad once when he'd nearly drowned. Will rolled her onto her back and covered her cold lips with his own. He blew into her and sat back. "Come back to me." He rubbed his arm across his mouth, diving back to blow more air into her. A faint rumble moved from deep inside Jonet, and she convulsed upward, water gurgling out of her. He tipped her to her side as more gushed from her lips. "Oh God, Jonet, aye." She started to cough, and he slapped her back some more.

There was movement above him. Stephen. He looked up to see Ewan and Searc leaping down from their mounts. Searc rushed to Nickum, who stood over Stephen while Ewan ran down to him. Jonet continued to cough and vomited. All signs of life. Thank the good, good Lord!

He ran his hands along her body. Bloody hell, where was Dory? Jonet could be bleeding inside.

Searc yelled something down to Ewan as he lifted Stephen across his horse. Ewan nodded and brought Bart over to where Will held Jonet, gently rocking her, supporting her while she fought for more breaths and spit water.

"Are ye hurt?" Ewan asked and tried to take Jonet from him, but he shook his head and held on. "Let me take her," Ewan said. "Ye're weakened from the fall."

His words made sense, but Will couldn't let go. "I can't. I won't let her go." The words echoed inside Will. *I won't let her go. I can't let her go.* When he'd seen her go over the falls…his reality had paused. Nothing else had mattered, only Jonet's life, as if his own depended on her very breath. He'd never felt anything so deadly before, so fatal to his own being. "I can't let her go," he said again and shook his head at Ewan.

Ewan stared back at him a long moment and finally nodded. "Let's get ye both on that horse then. Searc has the boy. That dog of his caught yer scent or the boy's. Led us here." He helped Will onto Bart's back. Will's muscles screamed, and he felt several gashes in his leg and along his hairline. Some of the wetness dripping down his forehead felt warm instead of icy cold. Ewan handed Jonet up to Will, who cradled her in front of him and climbed upon his horse. He led Bart back down the mountain trail in the near-blinding darkness.

Will held Jonet against his warmth. Even though they were both soaked, his body gave off heat, surrounding her. He glanced at Ewan in front of him. "How did you do it?" Will's voice was strained, and his throat ached.

"What?" Ewan asked, his voice grim.

"Watch Dory walk out of your life in the Tower."

Ewan guided them around several trees before he answered. "If she died, there was no reason to live." He looked back at Will. "How did ye jump off an unfamiliar waterfall in pitch-darkness?" He turned back around, the sound of the rushing water fading into the eerie silence of the forest. "Love makes a man do crazy or brave things, depending on how ye look at it."

Love? Did love hurt this much? Will could hardly breathe as he concentrated on the telltale signs that Jonet was still alive. Every breath from her lips allowed him to inhale, but she lay limp in his arms. He watched the moonlight infuse her face with white as they broke from the forest. She looked like death.

"Go," Will urged and tugged back the reins from Ewan. "I need to get her to Dory." He had to save her. If she died… "Now!" Will flew through the night as if death chased him, because it did. If Jonet died, his heart would surely stop.

· · ·

Cold, so cold… Then heat, burning her… Pain rasped

through her chest… A deep exhaustion dragged Jonet's limbs down as if she were indeed lost in the blackness of the swirling water, but instead of ice, she felt perfectly warm. Her eyelids lay heavy, unmoving, and she drifted in the darkness. Words and voices came together, some Gaelic, some English with strange accents. A familiar, deep timbre that made her heart race crept across the surface, always there even if she couldn't understand. The warmth of the comfortable darkness pulled her back down. Jonet slept.

The darkness turned reddish, a soft glow with movement in it.

"So, Will Wyatt is dead," a man said, finishing with a chuckle.

Nay! He couldn't be dead. If he was dead…she couldn't survive it. Will? She started to breathe fast. "Nay," she rasped and forced her eyes to blink. "Will?"

"She's moving," said a woman. "Did she say something?"

Jonet blinked, her fingers grabbing along warm wool. "Will?"

"She said your name." The first man chuckled. "'Tis a good thing she remembers you. Pete once was hit so hard on the noggin, he didn't know who he was for months."

"I'm here." The voice was warm near her ear, and she realized she was being held. "Wake up, Jonet."

Jonet's eyed flickered open, and she immediately saw the warm fire before her in a large hearth. A group stood around her, peering closely. But she didn't see Will.

She blinked. "Will?"

"Right here," he said behind her. "I've got you." He shifted her on his lap so she could see him.

"Ye're not dead," she whispered and cleared her throat.

"She's reopening her airway," Dory said as she touched her arm. "She's healthy, just waking from a shock."

"Nay, I'm not dead," Will said.

"But someone said ye were."

"That was me." Will's father stepped into view with a large grin. "We found two dead blokes and reported them as being Will and Ewan so no one can arrest them to get a bounty. They're already dead and being torn apart in London. Bloody royals."

He continued, "He can grow a broad beard, cut his hair, and take on a new name. I'm thinking he looks like a Geoff or Jack perhaps." He laughed.

Jonet stared up into Will's eyes. She managed to raise her hand, breathing fully again, and touched his face. "I like yer small beard and longish hair. And I love…yer name."

"I'm ready to go whenever you are," said Stephen, who appeared next to Captain Bart. Jonet began to push up, and Will helped her. She was wearing dry clothes, and they sat before the fire in the great hall at Munro Castle. Ann stood close and wiped at her eyes. She squeezed Jonet's hand. Searc and Caden, Donald and Gavin, Meg and Rachel, and Dory all watched her carefully.

"Stephen's well," she whispered.

"Aye," Will said, "but he'll be scrubbing decks and helping Pete in the kitchens for a year after that foolish, idiotic, stupid act."

The boy flushed and stepped back into the small crowd. "I'll follow him," Searc said. "Not taking any more chances."

"I think Nickum has taken to following him, too," Meg said. "Scared the boy terribly last night."

"How long have I been asleep?" Jonet said and tried to

stand, but Will held her in his lap. So she stayed.

"The night, a day…another night," Will said, and she studied his face. Dark circles stained under his eyes, his hair sat in tangles as if they'd dried with mud still in them. He must have held her the whole time.

"I'm well. Ye can let me down," she whispered.

He shook his head. "I can't let you go." He glanced up at the small crowd. "Dory, get Captain Bart some of that Highland whisky." His sister looped her arm through his father's and the group moved over to the far side of the room where Charissa sat on Margery's knee and laughed at Searc's dog as it chased its own tail.

"Ye need to clean yerself up," she said to Will. "Have ye been holding me this whole time?"

He looked back at her. "Ann changed you into dry clothes, and I changed, too."

"But then ye sat here with me?"

He nodded once. "Dory healed you, but you weren't waking up." Jonet felt his hands squeeze her where they held around her back and her legs. "She said you had to wake on your own, that the water in your lungs had been bad—"

"Ye saved me, went over the falls after me, didn't ye?" He nodded again once. "Bloody hell, Will, ye could have died."

"And you would have if I hadn't gone over," he said and sat her up. He rubbed his chin and down his face. He looked aged from worry or lack of sleep. "And then possibly anyways except that Dory saved you or Meg or Rachel. God's teeth, they all flashed their blue light over and through you."

She felt him shiver. "It was…bloody, swiving hell, Jonet," he rasped and pulled her closer. "I thought…I thought I'd lost you. I've never been scared before—never, not even when I was alone in that ship's hull. But when you wouldn't wake… I wouldn't let them take you away from me."

Jonet pulled closer to him and gave him a sweet, warm kiss. "But we're both alive." The words, though wonderful, also reminded her. "Unless ye go back to yer ship. Then Will Wyatt is dead," she whispered.

He looked closely into her eyes. The deep brown of his orbs were shot with rays of gold. She studied them, memorizing them. "You're right," he said slowly. "If I go back to the *Queen Siren*, if I leave you here, I will die."

She shook her head, her eyes narrowed in confusion. She opened her mouth to say something, but he stopped her. "And you can't go to sea, Jonet. It is too dangerous, especially without Dory there to heal you if anything happens. I can't… stand the thought of you being hurt, of you dying. So, there's just one thing that can happen."

She held her breath and waited.

A small grin caught at his lips, turning the serious, dark expression into one that she recognized. "I was rather hoping to honor my pledge to you, Jonet Montgomery." His grin turned into a smile. "I can start with building that new roof on the orphanage, but I believe there was another part to my oath. I seem to remember something about a lifetime of servitude."

Jonet couldn't breathe. Tears welled in her eyes. He caught one on his thumb as he continued, "You are the most caring, honest, beautiful person I've ever met. When I thought I'd lost you," his grin faltered, "well hell, I won't lose you again. So I'd like to shackle you to me." He nodded and smiled. "For life."

"Shackle?" she asked, her voice a little squeak.

"Aye, I believe folks call it getting wed."

The tears blurred her vision as Jonet lunged for Will's neck, wrapping him in a hug and kissing his cheeks, his once-broken nose, the scar down the side of his face. He chuckled and brought her face level with his. "Is that a yes?"

"Aye," she said. "I accept yer offer, Will Wyatt, a lifetime of servitude and shackled to me for life."

"Shall that be part of the vows?" he asked.

She brushed his lips with hers. "Most definitely."

"I love you, Jonet." He kissed her gently. "I didn't even know what it was before, thought it was a foolish notion, perhaps real for some, but not for me."

She kissed his lips, stroking his hair back from his handsome face. "And I love ye, my scoundrel pirate," she said.

"Aye, wench," he answered and smiled, a wicked glint in his eyes. "Ye may have tamed me into love, but together our hearts will always be wild." He leaned forward over her and slanted her head to deepen the kiss. It warmed Jonet's heart, and she knew with Will, she would never be cold again.

Epilogue

"Bart will be fine," Will said as he and Jonet rode along the pebbled path.

"His name is Bartholomew," Jonet corrected. "We did not name our son after a horse."

Will laughed. "Well, Captain Bart is often called a horse's arse." He hugged his lovely wife's arms to his chest as they swayed together in the saddle. "Either way, he will be fine. Aunt Dory is keeping him safe."

"Dory and Ewan have their own bairn to worry over."

"She keeps Bartholomew and Caroline together," Will said, "Margery helps, too, and Charissa feels like it's her responsibility to follow after her toddling brother."

Jonet sighed against his back. "I know. I just hate leaving them."

"All adventures from home start with a bit of sadness,

but you'll enjoy our trip on the sea," he said. He could almost smell the ocean breeze already. It had been two years since they had wed, two thrilling years of adventurous loving and living. Their son had been born nine months after their vows and had just weaned completely to solid food. It was the perfect time for them to travel before Will got her with child again.

"Charissa and Bartholomew will just laze about without me there to prod them. Margery is staying with them, but will she make certain they are helping Dory with the other children? I've left Dory with so much to do."

"Woman, you worry too much. They are all perfectly happy running your beautiful orphans' home." Will chuckled. "Meg will have them planting flower boxes and stringing blooms to make the cheery inside even prettier for those lucky little ones you've given a home. Dory will divide the chores between the older girls, including taking care of Bart...Bartholomew. Little Caroline wants to be there all day anyway. Dory said she thinks it's her home since it shares her name—Caroline Brody Home for Loved Orphans."

"Well, they are both named after Ewan's mother, a tribute to a brave and loving protector of children," she said and smiled. "Speaking of protectors of children, 'twill be good to see yer father." She tipped her head back, letting the sun shine on her face. "And Stephen. I hope the lad is finding his place in the world."

Will watched the sides of the path for some time, marveling at the green beauty in this land that he was starting to think of as his own. It was raw and unpredictable just like the sea and could swallow the unwary without a second thought. Aye, the world was a wondrous place.

"Are ye sure ye don't miss it?" she asked softly against his back.

"Ah, the freedom of the sea," he said wistfully and felt her stiffen. He kept his chuckle inside. "And the moldy bread, the smell of human waste at port, sleeping with a bunch of stinky men in hammocks, the cannibals who don't like to share their fruits, pissing off the bow. Ah, so much to miss."

She laughed and batted at his arm. He let Bart continue to plod along the path as he pulled Jonet to sit in front of him in the saddle.

"Ye know ye can't ride long like this," she reminded him and rubbed into his body. "I'll drive ye insane with lust." She stared at him wantonly.

He growled in her ear. "There's no hurry to get there. The captain knows we have to deliver Dory's package first. It could take another week. Perhaps we'll make camp early this eve."

She giggled as he nuzzled her ear. "Ye packed the box; ye're sure?"

Will reached to the leather bag strapped to the back of Bart. His fingers easily felt the wooden container, dubbed Pandora's box, after the fabled box that held all the evils in the world. Right now it held the Tudor rose ring that had been given to Dory by her mother.

Word had reached Druim of the search for the Wellington Witch, the name Dory had been burdened with after her escape from London. Ewan and Dory had decided it was time to let King Henry VIII know that they had indeed found the traitor in his court, fulfilling their obligations to the thorny monarch. Maybe then he wouldn't care that Dory and Ewan still lived.

The traitor would be unveiled since the ring was inscribed with the crafty bastard's name. Even though the man no longer posed a threat to Henry and his princesses, the man had continued the hunt for Dory, thus prompting her to reveal his traitorous past. It was his own quest to save himself that would lead to his doom.

"No worries. I wouldn't forget it." Will turned back to his love. "We'll send it through the boy Dory saved from poison at court and then head to the port at Barry where the *Queen Siren* waits. Then off to exotic lands."

"Islands with grapes and coconuts?" she asked blissfully.

"Aye," he nuzzled her neck, "and there's a certain little book that I plan to borrow from Adela."

Jonet gasped and laughed as Will pounced.

Did you love this Edge? Check out more of our titles!

And for exclusive sneak peeks at our upcoming books, excerpts, contests, chats with our authors and editors, and more...

Be sure to like us on Facebook

Follow us on Twitter

From the Author...

As an outspoken ovarian cancer survivor, I always list the symptoms of this sneaky, vicious disease in hopes that if you are experiencing any of them every day for more than three weeks, you will please go see your doctor.

Symptoms of Ovarian Cancer:

Bloating that is persistent

Eating less and feeling fuller

Abdominal pain

Trouble with your bladder

Ovarian Cancer cannot be detected by a PAP Smear. Additional symptoms may include fatigue, indigestion, back pain, pain with intercourse, constipation, and/or menstrual irregularities.

For more information about ovarian cancer, please check out the National Ovarian Cancer Coalition at www.ovarian.org.

About the Author

Heather McCollum is an award winning, historical paranormal romance writer. She earned her B.A. in Biology, much to her English professor's dismay. She's a member of Romance Writers of America and the Ruby Slippered Sisterhood of 2009 Golden Heart finalists.

When she is not creating vibrant characters and magical adventures on the page, she is roaring her own battle cry in the war against ovarian cancer. Ms. McCollum recently slayed the cancer beast and resides with her very own hero & 3 kids in the wilds of suburbia on the mid-Atlantic coast. For more about Ms. McCollum, please visit www. HeatherMcCollum.com.

Sign up for our Steals & Deals newsletter and be the first to hear about 99¢ releases from other fantastic Entangled authors!

Reviews help other readers find books. We appreciate all reviews, whether positive or negative. Thank you for reading!

Also by Heather McCollum

CAPTURED HEART

Healer Meg Boswell is running from the man who falsely accused her mother of witchcraft. Cursed with magical healing abilities, Meg knows that if she's caught, she will die atop a blazing pyre. Chief Caden Macbain is not above using an innocent woman to bargain for peace. He captures Meg, but she isn't who he thinks, and when she kills a man to save the clan, he must choose between duty and her life. For although he captured her to force peace, Meg's strength and courage have captured Caden's heart.

TANGLED HEARTS

Highland warrior Ewan Brody always wanted a sweet, uncomplicated woman by his side, but he can't fight his attraction to the beautiful enchantress who's stumbled into his life. He quickly learns, though, that Pandora Wyatt is not only a witch, but also a pirate and possibly a traitor's daughter—and though she's tricked him into playing her husband at King Henry's court, he's falling hard. As they discover dark secrets leading to the real traitor of the Tudor court, Ewan and Pandora must uncover the truth before they lose more than just their hearts.

HIGHLAND HEART

Alec Munro, chieftain of the Munros, has captured the Englishman who swindled his father. Set on retribution, he's caught off-guard by the thief's beautiful daughter, a lass whose beauty and spirit leave him questioning the value of revenge. Rachel Brindle must use her cunning and her healing magic to prevent the same slaughter that started the blood feud between two clans a century ago. But when her secret is exposed, will it condemn her in the eyes of the barbarian who has captured not only her family, but also her heart?

Experience more historical romance with these Entangled titles…

THE DUKE'S QUANDARY
by Callie Hutton

London 1814…

Drake, Duke of Manchester, has everything planned. This season he'll marry a woman who will be the perfect duchess and a docile wife. Then he's introduced to Penelope Clayton, the socially awkward houseguest his family has tasked him to prepare for the ton. Each lesson draws them closer, and he finds himself unable to resist her. But society can be cruel, and social expectations have a way of making decisions for you.

ONCE UPON A WALLFLOWER
by Wendy Lyn Watson

When Mira Fitzhenry's guardian arranges her engagement to one of the most scandalous, yet devastatingly handsome lords to ever grace the peerage, all of society is abuzz. After all, the man has left a trio of dead young women in his wake, including his first fiancée. As the wedding approaches, Nicholas and Mira grow ever closer, yet so does the very real danger. Will the truth bring Nicholas and Mira together or tear their love apart?

LOVE'S REVENGE
by Joan Avery

St. Louis, Missouri, 1879

The only things that have kept widower Stephen Worth alive for the past two years are the promise of revenge against the man who framed him for murder and the love for Andy, his son, who was taken by the beautiful but vexing sister of his dead wife. Now, full of desire for her, he must convince Kate to trust him before she learns the truth about his past—but his demons are all the ammunition she needs to keep his son for good.

AN UNEXPECTED SIN
by Sarah Balance

Colonial Salem

After losing everything once, Josiah Cromwell wants only to start over. He has come back to Salem…for Anne. He never forgot his hunger for her sensual curves, and the years have not faded the forbidden sensations. But Salem has become a world gone mad with fear and no one is safe from the trials and baseless accusations. Will Jacob and Anne's second chance for love come too late?

NO ORDINARY MISTRESS
by Robyn DeHart

London, 1814

Remington Hawthorne has spent his life protecting the Crown. When he's assigned to play the part of lover to Emma Masterson, he'll have to risk his heart as well as his life.

Perpetually tasked with proving she is as valuable as any man in her profession, the last thing Emma needs is to be reunited with the one man who makes her want to forget her duties and get lost in passion. It will take every ounce of strength not to give in to him…

TEMPTING BELLA
by Diana Quincy

Mirabella feels nothing but contempt for the man who wed her for her fortune and promptly forgot she existed.

Sebastian has been apart from his child bride since their wedding day. When he encounters an enchanting impish beauty at the opera, he's is thrilled to find she is none other than his long-ago bride and he is more than ready to make her his wife in truth.

Too bad the beguiling beauty has no intention of coming meekly to the marriage bed.

ONCE UPON A MASQUERADE
by Tamara Hughes

New York City, 1883

Self-made shipping magnate Christopher Black first spies Rebecca Bailey at a masquerade ball and is captivated by her refreshing naïveté and sparkling beauty. But when Christopher's investigation of the murder of his best friend leads him straight to Rebecca, he fears his ingénue may be a femme fatale in disguise. Now he must decide if he can trust the woman he's come to love, or if her secrets will be his downfall.

Printed in Great Britain
by Amazon